Abandoned

Lee Shepherd

First published 2015
By Rowanvale Books Ltd
2nd Floor
220 High Street
Swansea
SA1 1NW
www.rowanvalebooks.com

A CIP catalogue record for this book is available from the British Library.
ISBN: 978-1-910607-55-8

Chapter I

'Well done, Molly! Well done, sweetheart, that was absolutely fantastic.'

The father beamed after witnessing his eldest daughter take first place in a junior equestrian event. He, his wife and their youngest daughter, Fiona, stood among lots of other proud parents, most of whom were known to the family in their close knit community.

'Hi, Charles!'

The father turned to see who had called him. 'Oh hi, Mark! How's the wife and kids?'

'They're good thanks. I saw your Molly out there, she's really on her game today!'

'Yes, isn't she? We couldn't be prouder! Well, I'll see you at church on Sunday, okay?'

'Sure, see you!'

As Molly continued on her victory parade, soaking up the applause, she couldn't help but notice as she passed by her parents that her father's eyes were no longer on her as he was too transfixed checking his watch for the time.

Upon realising he was running late, Charles quickly glanced over at Molly and pointed to his watch, informing her that he would have to leave before she had even had time to collect her victory trophy and rosette. She couldn't help but drop her smile as she watched her father kiss his wife and her younger sister goodbye before waving one last time, then getting into his car and driving off. Her mother, seeing the disappointment in Molly's eyes, just offered a sympathetic smile and hug. She made sure to get some pictures of her receiving her rewards to show to her father upon his return from work that evening.

***

'Help! Help! Somebody, please help! Can anybody hear me? Please, if you can hear me, I beg you, please help! I don't know where I am, please somebody help me!'

The words pounded through the lone man's head as he calmly left, picking his way through the dense forest. He walked the four miles of the nature trail before making his way to his parked vehicle.

He casually drove away, without a second thought for the fifteen-year-old schoolgirl he had not long since abducted, tied up and abandoned in the six foot deep by eight foot wide underground cell he had earlier prepared. He grinned as he imagined her trapped inside with only a small ration pack and a bottle of water for company, forced to breathe through a thin ventilation pipe hidden by shrubbery. Alone in the dark without a phone and no clue to where she was.

Looking around blearily, still disorientated from her Ketamine-induced unconsciousness, panic started to settle into the girl's mind. She needed to get out — and fast.

***

Twenty minutes later, the man arrived back at his warm family home and was greeted by his wife, two young daughters and his border collie, Tess.

'Charles, darling! You're just in time for dinner.'

He and his family sat down at the table to say their prayers before tucking into their evening meal and discussing one another's day as a solid, loving family unit.

Once the meal had been consumed, the children politely asked if they may leave the table and go to their rooms to do their homework and prepare themselves for the evening. The girls were excused, and set about carefully folding and hanging their school uniforms before changing into their pyjamas and taking care of their homework assignments. Upon finishing, they then returned to the sitting room and settled down for the evening in front of the television. Molly's discontent at her father leaving earlier in the day still showed by the scowl on her face.

The parents, meanwhile, busied themselves with everyday household chores, taking care of the dishes, tidying up and doing whatever else needed done. Fiona was desperately trying to get their attention by singing and dancing in the centre of the living room, much to Molly's dismay.

'Sit down and shut up, Fi!' she snapped, jealous at the bond between her younger sister and their father.

Charles then decided to go out for his customary evening walk with Tess to get some fresh air and clear his head of the day's stresses and challenges, leaving the mother to do the laundry and arrange his veterinarian's uniform for the following day. As she did so she caught a glimpse of her younger self in a photo in the hall that showed her proudly standing in her old nurse's uniform; she paused for a second to think back on the career she had given up to raise their family. She then gently grasped the cross that hung around her neck, and thanked God for the life and family she had been blessed with before returning to her chores. Just an average day in the Lee household.

For all intents and purposes, everything appears to show a 'normal', well respected, loving family. Unbeknown to the ladies of the household however, everything was not as it appeared. Charles Lee had plenty of serious, unresolved issues and demons of his past; things he has never discussed with anybody till this day — not even his wife. Demons that he struggled with on a day to day basis, his mind a prison encasing all the torture, anger and frustrations of his childhood. He was hell bent on revenge, determined to have his pound of flesh. In doing so, he would inflict onto others the horrendous nightmares of his past, things that could have been so easily avoided if somebody had just bothered to listen to him and believe in him.

***

Mr Lee arrived back at the house after his walk with Tess to find the girls already in their bedrooms, settling in for the night. He visited each of their rooms and kissed them goodnight, then proceeded to read Fiona her favourite bedtime story while his wife, Rebecca, finished off the last of her endless chores.

'Charles, Charles, is that you?' Rebecca's voice came from down the hall.

'Be with you in a moment darling.'

He finished off his story to Fiona before tucking her in for the night, and by the time he had finished it was 9.30pm. Mr Lee then quickly checked his emails regarding tomorrow's schedule before finally settling down on the sofa in front of the television, sipping contentedly at the large glass of red wine his thoughtful wife had poured for him. The two of them then snuggled up together to watch some mindless programmes and unwind. Rebecca made Charles look through all the photos she had taken earlier in the day, beaming with pride at their triumphant eldest daughter's accomplishment, before retiring to bed.

Mrs Lee disappeared into the main bathroom to undress, leaving her husband to step into a nice hot shower in the en-suite bathroom.

Whilst the water washed over him, his mind wandered to the young girl he'd recently left behind. She'd be cold and alone, her limbs still not functioning properly due to the drugs he had injected her with. He could picture her lying, semi-naked, in a heap; he had torn off the majority of her clothes to reveal her firm young body. All of a sudden, he started to feel something he hadn't in months with his wife: he felt aroused.

The more he imagined how frightened and disorientated the girl would be, the more he pictured her sobbing and begging for help, the more aroused he became. Slowly, he started to touch himself, but before he'd even begun to start properly pleasuring himself, he heard Rebecca coming back into the room, shouting out for him to hurry up and get into bed for a 'cuddle', as she was cold in bed by herself.

Unbeknown to him, her real reason for wanting him to come to her was that she was lying in bed in a brand new matching underwear set and suspenders that she had recently purchased from Ann Summers; a desperate attempt to spice up their recently non-existent love life. Several times over the past few months, Charles has struggled to become aroused in bed; he had spurned his wife's advances on numerous occasions, blaming tiredness and the stresses of starting his own veterinary practice. In truth, he'd had far more than work on his mind.

He had secretly been seething with rage and repressed feelings of revenge. The perpetrators of the systematic torture and abuse he received as a child would have to pay.

This yearning for revenge was heightened by a chance encounter with one of his abusers just a few months earlier, after being called out to a farm near a small town named Wigton, just twelve miles outside of Carlisle in the Cumbrian Countryside. The farmer's prized cow had been attacked by either a fox or a badger, and the farmer was worried it may have contracted Tuberculosis. The farmer hadn't recognised the man standing before him, and why should he have? It had been nearly thirty years since he had last saw Charles as a withdrawn, scared fifteen-year-old boy. Charles, on the other hand, could never forget that puffed up, sweaty, red nosed, pockmarked face, nor the stench of whiskey which still clung to him as it did all those years ago. He never let on though; he remained as calm as he could manage, patched up the wound, then gave the cow a shot of antibiotics before making his escape.

After a short but erratic drive, he'd finally pulled into a layby on the way back and broke down in tears. Shaking and covered in sweat, with all the agonising memories he had repressed for so many years all flooding over him, he decided there and then that he wouldn't live the rest of his life in that shadow. Instead, he chose to face up to his past, and not bury it any longer.

***

Charles stepped out of the shower and dried himself off. He still felt aroused. Attempting to hide his semi-erect penis under his towel so as not to raise suspicion from Rebecca, he quickly jumped beneath the sheets. His mind was swiftly distracted from his own thoughts about the girl, instead focusing on the vision of his wife lying beside him, seductively looking at him and arching her back in a manner in which implied 'take me'.

Whether it was the thoughts he'd had whilst getting showered, or the look of his wife, or possibly a combination of both, she would never know, but that night, for the first time in ages, man and wife made love for the next hour or so and remembered what life used to be like. They remembered one of the reasons they fell in love in the first place. Once they had finished, they kissed each other goodnight, told each other of their love, then went to sleep in each other's arms — just like days of old.

Chapter 2

The next morning Charles woke surprisingly early, judging by the digits on his bedside clock; it was only 5.15am, but he was unusually alert for such an early start. He glanced over to where Rebecca lay and, seeing that she was still soundly sleeping, he gently got out of bed, grabbed his dressing gown from the back of the door, and quietly crept out of the bedroom, carefully closing the door behind him as not to rouse his sleeping wife. He padded to the kitchen to make himself his morning coffee.

Surprisingly, it wasn't the young girl in the forest that was on his mind this morning. For some reason all he could think about is Mr Beattie, the farmer whose cow he patched up not too long ago. Mr James Beattie, to give him his full title — Jim to his friends. Charles decided in that moment that he would pay him a visit today on the premise that he just wants to see how the animal is recovering. In reality, he was intrigued to know how somebody who committed such terrible acts towards children could so easily forget the face of a child who had trusted him and his wife to take them in as their own during their time as foster carers.

However, his thoughts quickly turned back to the girl. He tuned into the news channel on TV and was met by the image of her on the screen. The headline read, *fears grow for missing schoolgirl*. He turned up the volume to hear the reporter's words.

'I am standing here in the small town of Gretna, just on the Scottish border, where a community is in shock, praying for any news and the safe return of missing fifteen-year-old schoolgirl Lucy Mitchell after she disappeared late yesterday afternoon. She has not been seen or heard from since 5pm yesterday. Her parents and family are worried and are pleading for her to make contact and let them know she is safe.'

Then followed an emotional plea from her parents, Susan and Thomas Mitchell. The father spoke, as the mother seemed too distraught.

'Please, Lucy, if you are watching this and you are safe, please come home or let us know. We are not mad at you, we just want you home and to know you are ok.'

The camera was now back on the reporter.

'It is not yet known whether Lucy has run away from home, either with a boyfriend or someone she knows, and it is far too early to speculate if the situation is something more macabre, but the community is out in full force searching the area for any sign of her, or clues to her whereabouts. If anyone has any information regarding Lucy, could you please contact the police and let them know. This is Jennifer Metcalfe, reporting live from Gretna.'

Charles' thoughts now turned to sheer panic. What if somebody had seen him? What if he got caught? How would he explain this to his family? More importantly, what could he do about the girl? Then, as quickly as he had panicked, he remembered what he had learned in the army about staying calm under pressure, and carrying on under difficult conditions. He forced himself to relax and started to think other thoughts — darker, sinister thoughts. Fuck that little slag, she got what she deserved, the filthy little whore. Nobody is really going to grieve for that horrible little bitch, I'm doing the world a favour by taking sluts like that off the street!

He casually finished his coffee and proceeded to take his morning shower before getting dressed and preparing his daughters' breakfast. Rebecca came into the kitchen ten minutes later and was met by the aroma of porridge cooking on the hob and the smell of bread being toasted.

'Cup of tea, darling?' he asked her.

'I would love one, please. Why didn't you wake me?'

Charles shrugged. 'You just looked so peaceful sleeping, so I thought I would let you have a little longer this morning and prepare the girls' breakfast myself.'

'Ah, thank you very much, I feel much better for it, I must've needed it after last night's shenanigans, you big, hunky stud!'

She gave him a sly wink and a kiss on his cheek. This didn't go unnoticed by the girls, who were now sat at the breakfast table.

'Eurgh, gross!' Molly exclaimed. 'Get a room! I don't want to think of my parents being lovey-dovey, it's disgusting!'

Fiona, on the other hand, didn't really understand what was going on. This didn't stop her from jumping on the bandwagon anyway, trying to win respect from her older sister by copying her.

'Yeah, get a room you two!'

Charles just gave Molly a stern glance and left the room to go get his coat and shoes. Saying goodbye, he then headed towards the door to leave.

'Erm, aren't you forgetting something, mister?' Rebecca said huffily.

'Oh! Sorry, love.'

Charles returned to give his wife a kiss goodbye and inform her he will be running late tonight, as he had important business to sort out at the practice. With that, he got into his Volvo SUV and proceeded to head off up their long driveway and out onto the main road.

***

The narrow roads were quiet at this time in the morning, except for the occasional logging wagon moving back and forward from nearby Kielder forest. As he drove through the remote villages and countryside, he couldn't escape the image of the missing schoolgirl. A billboard outside a local shop clearly displayed the picture he had not long since seen on the news. This happened again as he passed through more villages. This was all a little bit too close to home for his liking — maybe he should have chosen his victim a little further afield. Ah well, it was a mistake he promised himself he wouldn't make again anytime soon.

Charles arrived at the practice and was met by Linda, his receptionist, who handed him a pile of envelopes before quickly running through the day's schedule. She needn't have bothered; his mind was not on his workload — he had his own agenda. He asked Linda to transfer his schedule over to one of his colleagues, stating that he has too many follow-up jobs to attend to. All lies of course, but that's the beauty of being the boss. Linda just agreed, and Charles retreated to his office.

The first thing he did was turn on the radio and tune into the local station CFM, desperate for more news on the girl — Lucy Mitchell. He hadn't particularly wanted to know her name, as it made her more human. The girl was just a dirty little slut, worthless and expendable. Lucy Mitchell has a family, friends — she was their darling loved one. This made him think of Fiona and, to some extent, Molly, but he tried not to let the thought of that happening to them and how he would feel enter his mind. He had a plan, he just needed to put it into action.

After an hour or so of reviewing client files, he takes out of the medical storage unit some bandages, syringes and bottles of sedatives and anaesthetic. Placing them in his bag, he left his office and the practice, telling Linda he had to go out and probably won't be back for the rest of the day. She thought this a little odd, but chose not to question him as he didn't seem himself today. He got back into his car and decided to take a drive back out to Wigton to see Mr Beattie at Haywood farm.

***

Upon arrival at the farm, he was a little taken aback as Mr Beattie rushed over to greet him.

'Hello, Mr Lee, what a pleasant surprise. To what do I owe the honour of your visit?'

'Er, it's just a courtesy call, Mr Beattie, to see how the old girl is holding up since I was last here. I just thought I would call in as I was in the area and passing by.'

'Well I'm so glad you did, come take a look at her — she's recovered remarkably well thanks to you, sir,' the farmer said eagerly. 'Less of the "Mr Beattie" please, would you? Friends call me Jim,' he added.

Charles was still taken aback by Jim's charm offensive. 'Ok, Jim,' he said weakly.

'Can I get you a drink, Mr — er sorry, I didn't catch your first name — Charles, wasn't it?'

'Yes, it's Charles, Jim. And a coffee would be great, thank you. Strong with sugar and milk please,'

'No problem, Charles, follow me, old boy.'

With that, they headed into the farmhouse. Glancing around the old fashioned kitchen/dining room, Charles caught a glimpse of an old photo of Jim standing next to who Charles knew to be Mrs Edna Beattie, a woman he harboured mixed feelings for. He loved her because she'd been kind to him and had showed him affection; she would often patch him back up after heavy beatings and drunken gang rapes from Jim and his pals. However, he also hated her for the fact that she'd allowed this to happen to him and covered up for Jim when Charles, who was then named Jonathon, tried reporting him to his

Social worker. They would both brush it off as though it was Jonathon who was the liar, because he didn't want to adhere to their strict Christian beliefs and hardworking ethics. The truth was, even though she knew what was going on, she was just as afraid of her husband as Jonathon was but, unbeknown to Jonathon, his Social worker was a member of the same Masonic lodge as Mr Beattie, and would never knowingly betray the trust of one of his brothers, so the abuse was allowed to continue for a number of years.

'So, do you live here alone then, Jim?' Charles asked, trying to keep his feelings in check.

'I'm afraid I do now, old chap,' Jim responded. 'Ever since the wife died from cancer a few years back, it's just me and the cows now.'

'I'm so sorry to hear that, Jim,' Charles responded. 'I'm sure she was a fine woman?'

'The best.'

The two of them sat and drank their coffee, exchanging conversation in a warm, pleasant manner, but all the while Charles remembered just how good Jim was at this game, leading you into a false sense of security with his apparent friendly nature, all the while hiding a dark, sinister, vicious side. A side that Charles had seen far too often growing up. Upon finishing his drink, Charles politely thanked Jim for his hospitality, said goodbye, opened the back door and walked back to his car, managing to maintain and control both his hatred towards the man and the overwhelming urge to kill him in his own home. Charles knew this wasn't the best situation, and would bide his time until the right moment presented itself. With that, he started his engine and drove out of the farm.

***

Charles could feel his heart racing as he drove back to Carlisle. With adrenaline surging through his body, his senses heightened and with revenge firmly set in his mind, he decided to bypass Carlisle and the practice altogether. Instead, he headed straight on and over the border as though he was heading home, although home couldn't be further from his mind at this moment in time. He passed back through Newcastleton, again seeing the young brunette's face all over the billboards. He continued on over the humpback bridge and, instead of turning left as he usually would, he went right up the quiet country road that led to Kielder water and forest park.

He parked his Volvo in a small, quiet layby, hidden away from the busy car parks used by visitors and locals alike, then reached over and grabbed the bag he'd prepared earlier. He then leant over to the glove compartment and removed his black leather driving gloves before exiting the vehicle, looking around nervously to ensure nobody was watching. With that, he jumped over a small broken-down fence and made his way into the thick, dense forestry that surrounded Northern Europe's largest manmade lake. He knew the forest well, due to him taking Tess, the family's Border collie, on many a long walk through it. He'd specifically chosen this particular spot as no paths or mountain bike trails ran through it; this outer circle was home to nothing but wildlife for miles around.

He proceeded to trudge through four miles of dirt, moss and branches, becoming more and more excited as he did so. He noticed the November sky darkening and glanced at his watch: 4.28pm. A smug grin curled across his face; he knew there was no rush to get home after forewarning Rebecca he would be late that evening. He took his phone out of his pocket and switched it off, not wanting any distractions. He would savour every moment of what was to come.

An eerie silence fell upon Charles as he approached the site of the makeshift dungeon.

Charles loved the secluded environment — here, he was in his element; he was far more comfortable and at one with nature than he ever was with other people. As he got nearer, he could hear a faint whimpering coming from under all the debris and earth that was camouflaging the padlocked chains over the thick, heavy wooden roof he had carefully and painstakingly locked into place to ensure there would be no chance of escape. He removed the branches and leaves scattered over the entrance.

'WHO'S THERE? PLEASE HELP ME, I'M TRAPPED DOWN HERE, SOMEBODY PLEASE HELP ME!'

Ignoring the girl's cries, Charles removed his keys from his pocket and unlocked the thick iron padlock, all the while scanning the area to be certain nobody else is around. He needn't have worried, as darkness was now cloaking his actions and nobody in their right mind would want to be out here now and risk becoming lost in this thick terrain. He slowly raised the wooden cove. As the last rays of daylight fall down into the small, dark chamber, he could barely make out the shadowy silhouette sat cowering in the corner, knees locked tight into her chest. She seemed to be shaking and shivering — both due to the cold temperatures her barely clothed body had been exposed to and due to sheer fear that had consumed her every thought for the past twenty-four hours. Her hands and feet were still bound with cable ties, while her fingers and hands were black from trying to tunnel her way out of the cold, hard winter earth, to no avail.

As he lifted the cover further, he noticed the pungent stench of ammonia filling his nostrils. Instead of having any sympathy for the young girl before him, another wry smile came upon his face at the thought of her having to sit in her own urine, and the degradation she'd been subjected to. This didn't repulse him; instead it excited him. He felt a stirring in his loins as he contemplated the power and control he held over his vulnerable young victim. Again, he felt adrenaline race through his body — his palms sweaty, his senses intensified. With a steely determination fixed firmly in his mind, he climbed down into the pit, advancing towards the petrified figure before him.

The girl backed quickly away from him, pressing herself into the side of the dungeon. 'WHAT DO YOU WANT FROM ME? LEAVE ME ALONE! WHO ARE YOU?'

Charles remained silent.

Reaching out, he grabbed her by her tatty hair and lifted her to her feet. Suddenly and swiftly, he delivered a single left hook that connected with her right cheek. Stunned and trying to regain her senses, the girl struggled to get to her feet in a last-ditch attempt to attempt an escape. Her efforts were futile as he struck another blow to her face, then proceeded to kick her to the ribs as she lay in the dank, dark dirt. Blow upon blow came down upon her body as she curled into the foetal position, whimpering, desperate to remain conscious. She begged for him to stop, but again he continued, engulfed in a rage-driven frenzy, and beat her to a blood-soaked pulp. She finally passed out in a heap, a million miles away from anything she had ever known, with no support from family or friends, totally alone and vulnerable to this monster of a man — completely at his mercy.

Charles climbed back up out of the pit and reached for his bag. He then removed a five-millilitre syringe barrel and needle and took out the bottle of Ketamine he had initially used to sedate her. Climbing back down to where she lay, Charles carefully administered the full contents of the syringe into her limp body. Any chance of her regaining her senses was now completely diminished, as the dose he had just given her is usually reserved for putting fully-grown horses to sleep.

Charles smiled in satisfaction. There would be no more screams or moaning from this one.

The bloodlust slowly took complete control over him. He looked down where she lay, his menacing blue eyes piercing the teenager's bloody, filth-stained body, the moonlight softly highlighting her faint young curves. Thoughts started whirring through his mind furiously. Was this what *she* looked like? Was this how his dirty little whore mother looked when she was lying on her back being impregnated at fourteen, before giving me up at birth? Dropping him like he was worthless? How he despised her! What kind of a person could do that to a baby? Who could abandon something as innocent as a new-born child?

His fury suddenly broke free as he raged to the heavens. 'FUCK YOU, MOTHER! FUCK YOU!'

With that, he got down on the ground and knelt between the girl's thighs. He glanced up at her face, noticing that her eyes pointed to the back of her head, oblivious to what was happening.

He was still uttering those words under his breath, 'Fuck you, fuck you, Mother!'

He pulled off her short skirt, then tore off her underwear with one swipe. His excitement was like nothing he had ever experienced as he proceeded to pull down his trousers. He wiped the beads of sweat from his forehead with his arm; he knew what he is about to do is wrong on every level, but he needed to make her pay. He needed her to feel exactly how he felt, to be helpless and at his mercy, just as he used to be at Mr Beattie's mercy.

His anger was mostly aimed at his biological mother for leaving him in the care of Social Services and the local authorities, the people that failed him on so many levels, the people who allowed the abuse, beatings and rapes to continue through incompetence and disbelief. He was angry at the life he never had, and the family he'd never known.

He climbed on top of his comatose victim, pausing for a second only to make sure her eyes were still shut, then proceeded to enter the girl. After only a couple of thrusts, he could feel himself nearing ejaculation, much to his disappointment as he wanted the moment to last. He reached out and placed his large, gloved hands around Lucy's limp neck and gently started to squeeze. He began to thrust harder and faster as he tightened his grip.

'FUCK YOU, MOTHER, FUCK YOU, YOU DISGUSTING LITTLE WHORE!' He spat the words out like venom.

Her face became redder as her blood vessels began to surface and burst; as he throttled her to the point of asphyxiation. Suddenly, just as he was about to climax, her eyes opened abruptly and looked up at the man on top of her. He caught her gaze, looking deep into her ever-dilating green eyes. She was nearing the point of death when something strange happened: a tear fell from his eye, landing on her dirt-ridden face. But it was too late, he knew he couldn't turn back, he couldn't undo what he had already done. With that, he increased the pressure considerably, but it wasn't profanities he was exclaiming anymore; instead he simply whispered down at her, 'I'm so sorry' right at the point of climax and, in that instance, Lucy Mitchell's young life was extinguished. Ended at the hands of this so-called 'family man' and 'loving father'.

Several seconds passed before he realised she'd gone; he was so lost in his own twisted euphoria. He quickly regained his senses and leant down to close her eyes before planting a soft kiss on her forehead.

'Goodnight, Mother...sweet dreams.'

He then casually climbed off of her to his feet, then pulled up his trousers and straightened up while wiping his tear-soaked eyes. His composure now restored, he reached up and pulled himself out of the pit. He nonchalantly looked over the body lying before him for a short while, then slammed the cover down, pulling the chains tight. He made doubly sure that the padlock was back in place before covering the entrance entirely with forest debris, shrubbery and leaves. To the unknown eye, nobody would ever know it was there.

The dark of night was well and truly present upon the thick, dense forest as he made his way back through the labyrinth of trees before him, carefully navigating his route, as he knew — more than anyone — just how unforgiving this terrain could be under the cover of darkness. He made his way out of the tree line, back over the fence towards his waiting Volvo. He double checked his person to make sure there were no clues to his secret macabre activities. As he did so, he noticed his boots were thickly covered in mud and moss, and blood splattered up the front of his wax jacket. This didn't bother him, however; he knew Rebecca was used to him coming home covered in blood and dirt from attending farms, delivering cattle and suchlike. It was the blood on his face that caught his attention as he looked in his rear view mirror. He pulled out his handkerchief and quickly removed it before placing his gloves back in the glove box, then carefully hid the bag he had prepared under the passenger seat. He composed himself again and concocted a story to relay to his wife. Satisfied, he pulled away from the layby and travelled the fifteen miles away from Kielder, heading back to the comfort of his own home, the warmth of his loving wife and children and the unconditional love of his beloved collie, Tess.

***

Back at the house, Rebecca greeted Charles with a loving embrace, thoughts of last night's intimacy still fixed firmly in her mind; secretly she hoped for more of the same tonight.

'So how was your day, love?'

'Same old, same old, dear. You know how it is, there are always sick animals to tend to,' Charles responded automatically.

She didn't pry any further, as she could see he looked tired. She simply just offered to run him a nice hot bath.

'That would be great. Thanks, dear. I'll just take Tess for a quick walk whilst you do so.'

With that, he headed back out of the door.

He looked forward to his evening walks with Tess, as he would make a habit out of talking to her about his problems and feelings; even though she didn't respond, he somehow felt as though they had a connection. He liked to believe she understood him on some level.

'I had to do it, Tess, I had to. She would've talked, she would've sent me away! She asked for it, but its ok now, she can't talk anymore, she's gone for good. It's just us again now, no more distractions.' Once he had finished offloading, they turned around and headed back to the house.

Upon their return, Rebecca had his customary glass of red wine poured ready for him, and announced that his bath was ready. 'Just be quiet,' she warned, 'as the kids have not long gone to sleep.'

He thanked her then headed to the bathroom, where he removed his filthy clothes before proceeding to relax in the hot, tranquil bath before him. He drank his wine, scrubbed any trace of DNA from his body, then just lay there, lost in his own little world, a twisted sense of justice and justification engrossing him. He was proud of what he'd accomplished. The realisation that he was capable of exerting that dominance and control over another human being, and inflicting the ultimate punishment, not only excited him, but empowered him. The feelings of being lost, helpless, and at the mercy of others as a child no longer held weight in his mind; for once, he had the power and control — and he loved it!

Forty minutes passed before Rebecca came and knocked on the bathroom door.

'You ok in there?'

'Yeah, just getting out now, love,' said Charles, snapping out of his reverie.

'Ok', she replied. 'I'll just be in the living room.'

He put on his dressing gown that hung on the back of the door, picked up the pile of clothes in front of him and took them to the kitchen, loading them straight into the washing machine. He set the controls to a boil wash, inserted the powder, and pressed start. He relaxed a little, pouring himself another large glass of wine, finishing off the bottle by doing so. He found Rebecca waiting for him in the lounge, but, ignoring her, he sat on the couch, took control of the remote control and turned on the news channel.

About fifteen minutes or so of national news headlines appeared on screen before it got to the regional news. They showed footage of flooding around the west Cumbria area before finally getting to the news of the missing girl.

'Still there is no news on missing Lucy Mitchell...'

Charles is somewhat pleased by this, but Rebecca seemed less so.

'Have you seen this Charles? It's terrible. That poor girl's family must be devastated. Gretna is only forty minutes from here. I couldn't bear it if that was to happen to one of our girls, I'd be beside myself.'

Charles just mumbled, 'Yeah, me too,' on autopilot, as he was too engrossed in what was happening on screen.

The news finally came to an end. Downing his drink, Charles got up.

'I'm off to bed. Work's exhausted me today,' he announced.

Rebecca seemed a little miffed — perhaps she was hoping that last night's passion might have unlocked some of the old spark from their relationship. However, she pecked him on the cheek in forgiveness; after all, he was a hardworking man that provided a good stable life for the family.

'Ok dear, I'll be through shortly, goodnight,' she said, and looked at him wistfully as he turned away.

Just a simple 'goodnight' was thrown over his shoulder as he exited the room. He stopped at Molly's room first, entering and making sure she was tucked in. Placing a kiss on her head, he bade her goodnight and then entered Fiona's room to do the same, taking extra care to ensure she had her favourite teddy bear to cuddle — she hated to wake up without it beside her. He then took himself off to bed where, surprisingly, whether by some sort of the adrenaline comedown or his sheer lack of conscience, he fell into a deep sleep within minutes of resting his head.

Chapter 3

The next morning, Charles was awoken by the bright winter sun shining through the curtains and upon his face. He looked over at the clock, and as usual it read 5.15am. Without work to get up for, as the practice was shut on Saturdays, he just lay there. Everyone else in the household was still sound asleep, so the house was silent. He thought of Lucy, about how she would probably thank him and be grateful for him taking her life, a life that would have probably been nothing but misery and suffering; how she must have enjoyed sharing her final moments in his embrace. He believes he saw in her dying eyes a moment of clarity and understanding, and in that moment she had realised the reasons for his actions and how lucky she had been that he had chosen her.

His narcissism was now in full flow, consuming his every thought. He looked over at Rebecca lying beside him, fully engrossed in his warped fantasy and his heightened sense of arousal. He placed his hand under the Egyptian cotton sheets and ran it down his wife's side, from her ribs, down past her waist and over her hips. He then proceeded to raise her silk camisole and gently run his fingers over her pubic bone and inside her black French knickers. He moved in closer; by now he noticed the slight hint of Jasmine and Eucalyptus scent wafting from her recently washed mousey hair combined with the sweet scent of her favourite Chanel perfume.

She slowly awoke, her back still turned to him, as he began to massage her clitoris, pressing his erect penis into the small of her back. She didn't let on that she was awake, but chose instead to let him carry on until she felt herself become more and more aroused. By this point, she could feel the warm dampness building inside of her and arched her back towards him, pressing her firm buttocks into his groin in a submissive manner, but still not saying a word.

Charles needed no further encouragement; he entered her now lubricated vagina and steadily began to build up a rhythm whilst caressing her breasts and nipples. She let out little gasps of encouragement as he gained pace, happy to be reconnecting with her recently-distant husband, hoping this was the start of a turning point in their marriage.

Charles, on the other hand, slowly became more and more submerged in his own thoughts as the lines between fantasy and reality became more and more blurred. He ran his left hand up the front of her body, over her erect nipples, and placed it softly around her neck, all the while still caressing her with his right hand. He slowly started to tighten his grip as he continued to penetrate her. She didn't mind at first, although this is something he had never done before. She just chose to go along with it; if truth be known, it was secretly turning her on. She could feel a build-up of pressure inside herself as she gradually approached orgasm. Charles began to thrust harder; instead of his loving wife in front of him, all he saw was Lucy as he became more and more animalistic and forceful with each thrust.

Rebecca was now right on the edge of climax and let go of herself, shuddering in intense orgasm. Charles tightened his grip even further around her neck as he reached the point of no return. By this point, Rebecca was struggling to breathe and tried to gently encourage him to loosen his grip, not wanting to make an issue of it while he was still not done. It was no use though; he squeezed her throat even harder, and in that moment he shuddered in an equally intense climax before coming back to his senses and releasing his grip from her neck. He knew from her face that he went too far, and knew she was going to question him about it, but in that moment they both just lay there in silence — her, baffled and shocked by what just happened, and him, revelling in his masculinity and sexual prowess.

Right at that moment, before Rebecca could utter a word about what had just happened, Fiona came bursting in the door.

'Daddy, Daddy, can we still go shopping today? You promised, you promised.'

'Of course we can, sweetheart,' he replied. 'Now, come and tell me all about your week. How's school been? Have you been good?'

Whilst Fiona began to tell her father all about what had been happening at school and about her friends, Rebecca got up out of bed and turned to face Charles.

'Would you like a cup of coffee, darling?'

'That would be lovely, thanks, dear.'

He turned back to Fiona, listening all about the weekly events in his youngest daughter's life. Who was popular, who wasn't, who'd been naughty and who was doing what this weekend. He sat and listened intently and thought to himself how lucky he was to have such a wonderful young daughter and loving family.

Rebecca, meanwhile, was in the kitchen making herself and Charles a nice big mug of freshly ground coffee. Still a little taken aback, she caught a glimpse of her reflection in the mirrored fridge edging; she had several red finger marks around her throat still. Oh, what would people think if they are to turn into bruises? She wasn't best pleased. Turning up the collar on her dressing gown so as to hide the marks from Fiona's inquisitive young nature, she returned to the bedroom with their drinks.

'Fifi, darling,' she said, 'why don't you go and wake your sister? Get washed and dressed, both of you —

we have a long day ahead of us today and we don't want to be late.'

Charles, sensing a tone in her voice, reaffirmed this and told Fiona, 'Do as your mother says dear, we'll be up soon.'

They waited quietly until Fiona had left the room and closed the door firmly behind her.

'Is something wrong, dear?' Charles asked his wife, totally oblivious to the covered marks around her neck.

Rebecca faced an internal struggle: she was still not best pleased, but on the other hand she didn't want to rock the boat and turn it into a big deal — she was happy to have some intimacy back in their lives, and partly because she was slightly confused and baffled by how much it secretly turned her on.

She folded down her collar, pointed to her neck, and asked him in a half-joking, half-serious manner, 'What do you call this, mister? Look at the state of my neck, I look as though I barely got away from the Boston strangler!'

'Oh, bloody hell, love!' he exclaimed. 'I don't know what came over me. I'm sorry, I must have got carried away in the heat of the moment. I certainly didn't mean to hurt you, or mark you for that matter.'

'Well don't let it happen again, or there will be big trouble! Or at least not so bloody hard next time anyway!' She gave him a teasing little grin and wink, then proceeded to lay down on the bed next to him, glad that the elephant was now out of the room.

The couple then took turns to get showered and dressed before sitting down and having breakfast with their daughters.

Charles looked up at Molly sitting across the breakfast table and shook his head; she was totally absorbed in whatever app she had on her mobile phone that particular day. Her music was blasting from her headphones, and he struggled to hold any sort of conversation with the others.

'Molly', he said sternly. She didn't hear him due to the loud music and still stared down at her phone. 'MOLLY!'

This time she heard him, and looked up to catch his gaze. She could see that he clearly wasn't happy.

Casually removing one of her headphones from her ears, she asked, 'What?'

Her attitude angered her father. 'DON'T YOU "WHAT" ME, YOUNG LADY! For once, would you take out them damn headphones, pay more attention, and actually make an effort to be involved in family conversations.'

'Whatever,' Molly muttered under her breath — a small show of defiance. However, she removed the other headphone and placed the phone in her pocket. She didn't want to anger her father any further; if she tried to stay in his good books, he would be more inclined to buy her the new outfit she'd secretly been hoping for.

'Thank you.'

His voice seemed calmer and his blood pressure was slowly returning to normal. Drama over, the family then continued to finish their breakfasts and engage in casual chit-chat around the table. Once they'd all finished, Charles stood up.

'Right, I'm taking Tess for her walk.' Taking his coat from its stand, he put on his boots and left the girls to tidy up whilst he escaped the house, eager to clear his head with his trusted companion beside him.

Upon his return, Molly greeted him with a big hug and said, 'I'm sorry, Daddy!' before he could even get through the door and in out of the cold.

'It's ok, sweetheart, maybe I overreacted slightly. I just want you to engage more with us, I miss my little girl. Just don't be in a rush to grow up so fast.'

'I won't, Daddy, I promise.' It was too late though, as Charles knew that his once little princess and apple of his eye, was quickly growing into a young lady right before his eyes, and that worried him, as more and more recently her talk had been all about boys, as opposed to her usual school and equestrian talk. He was beginning to fear that she may go off the rails and end up down the same path as his biological mother: a terrifying thought.

As the family clambered into the car, ready to leave, Charles said, 'Change of plans guys.'

They all turned and looked at him, slightly confused, wondering what was going on.

'I've decided that instead of shopping in Carlisle today, how would you all like to go to the Metro Centre at Gateshead instead?'

The two girls instantly got excited by this.

'Yeah, Dad, can we? Can we?'

He turned and smiled at Rebecca sat beside him.

'Of course we can girls,' he said, grinning still. 'And you can pick anything you want, within reason of course.'

'YAY!'

Off they drove for a day out as a whole family unit — a rare thing these days, since Charles had spent so much time building up the practice for the past eighteen months.

'So why the change of plans?' Rebecca asked her husband, as the journey got underway.

'No reason, darling,' he lied. 'Just thought it would make for a nice day out for the girls, and a pleasant change for us.'

Again she just looked at him and smiled, happy in her blissful little bubble, totally unaware that the man she loved had a darker side.

Of course, he had only changed his plans as the route they now followed ran right past Kielder, and gave him a chance to double-check that there wasn't any activity or police interest. Plus, more importantly, it gave him a chance to secretly gloat at his own magnificence, irrespective of his family in the car with him.

Chapter 4

Over the next few days a sense of normality ensued. Charles returned to running the practice, Molly and Fiona went back to school and Rebecca continued to do what she did best: she kept the house in order, took care of her family and Tess and organised parish events.

Things were finally starting to look up for the family after months of uncertainty and stress due to the long hours Charles was putting into building up and establishing his own veterinary surgery. It had been worth it; the surgery was something he'd always dreamed of doing ever since he was a young boy, when his adoptive parents had got him a black springer spaniel puppy, Toby, for Christmas. He'd always felt an unconditional love and understanding towards animals which he'd never felt for people. However, he found himself becoming more and more dismayed by his profession; he had become a vet to try and help animals, yet seemed to spend the majority of his working week euthanizing sick cattle and domestic pets alike.

Marring this newfound happiness, however, was the continued hunt for the missing schoolgirl, Lucy Mitchell. Her disappearance was still very much prevalent in the local news, and every now and then Charles would see the same lead journalist Jennifer Metcalfe on his TV screen, reporting from Gretna. He wasn't worried; with every day that passed, the likelihood of her being found decreased, and there didn't appear to be any leads to her whereabouts. It was as if she'd just disappeared without a trace. This pleased Charles, as he could now concentrate solely on his work and family, his delusional hate-fuelled appetite sated for the time being. With Christmas only three weeks away, he would have plenty of things to occupy himself with.

***

Days soon turned into weeks and, as Christmas drew ever nearer, the hunt for Lucy seemed to have tapered off, as if the police, media, and authorities had given up hope of her ever turning up unscathed. Charles thought privately they must have resigned themselves to the fact that they had been outwitted and outsmarted by a far superior opponent, and had abandoned all hope of ever finding her. He revelled in the fact that he now appeared to be in the clear; and he could finally relax, take some time off work, and enjoy all the season's festivities safe in the knowledge that nobody would ever become aware of his disturbing secret life.

Charles had mixed feelings about this time of year — not due to his Christian beliefs, but more to do with the fact that when everybody else was enjoying this joyous time, Charles knew that Mr Beattie liked to invite his friends from the lodge round over the Christmas period. This meant that large amounts of alcohol were consumed, which always went hand in hand with the abuse he sustained. He vividly remembered waiting, terrified, for the men to take it in turns to visit his bedroom and use him as if he was an extra present laid out for them as part of Mr Beattie's hospitality.

Christmas also brought back fond memories of a distant part of his life, in particular, the first six years, when he'd celebrated Christmas in the McMullen household. Mr William McMullen, and Mrs Victoria McMullen were a working-class couple from

Whitehaven in West Cumbria, who, after struggling to conceive for several years, were finally given the news that they would never be able to bear children together: William was infertile. Undeterred, this just brought the already solid couple even closer, and they decided to go down the adoption route. Eventually, they took in and named the five-week-old boy before them as Jonathon William McMullen. This had been the only true family he had ever known — the only time in his childhood he ever felt loved and safe.

Chapter 5

It was on the evening of August 10th 1972 that a young expectant mother by the name of Shelley Winter was admitted into Workington's West Cumberland Infirmary. Escorted by her parents and a midwife, she was led straight into the maternity ward, as she was already in the first stages of labour. In agony, gasping through her tears, the girl spent the next eight hours surrounded by only her midwife, several doctors and the disapproving looks of her devout Jehovah's Witness parents.

She finally gave birth — without any pain relief due to her parent's beliefs — to a healthy baby boy at around half past four in the morning, weighing in at 7lb 2oz. The midwife immediately cut the umbilical cord, wrapped the boy in a blanket and passed him to his exhausted mother.

'Have you decided what you are going to name him?'

Before Shelley could utter a word, her father piped in, 'NO! SHE'S ALREADY BROUGHT ENOUGH SHAME ON THIS FAMILY WITHOUT NAMING THIS FATHERLESS BASTARD!'

The midwife, shocked by this reaction, could not even find any words to respond to the father. She just threw him a disgusted look, then turned to where Shelley lay with her new-born son.

'I'll leave you to bond with your son for a few minutes, Shelley,' she said kindly, 'then I will get him all cleaned up for you.'

Shelley could see the genuine sincerity in her

eyes, and the pure disgust at her father's words. 'Thank you.'

She then turned her attention to the innocent child in her arms, fresh tears appearing down her cheek. She knew these precious few hours would be the only time she would ever get to be so close to him, and even through the exhaustion, she clung onto him as tight as she could without hurting him until the midwife returned.

The next few hours seemed to pass by like minutes for Shelley as she just sat there, staring at the now sleeping boy wrapped in a fluffy woollen blanket in the glass crib next to her. Engrossed in her own thoughts, and totally dismissive of her parents close by, she was suddenly alerted to a portly middle-aged gentleman as he entered the room and made his introductions to the parents. What happened next all seemed surreal and like a blur to young Shelley.

'Seeing as you are under the age of sixteen, the age of legal consent, your parents have signed the voluntary consent forms on your behalf. This in turn means that your baby will now be placed into the care of the Social Services until a suitable long-term alternative is discovered. Do you understand what this means, Shelley?'

She knew exactly what this meant. Her parents had informed her of this decision and had reaffirmed it over the last two months. They had only found out about her hidden pregnancy at six months, as she knew if they had known in the early stages, they would have made her abort the unborn child without anybody ever having to find out. Their only saving grace now was the fact that nobody apart from the people in that room had any inclination of her ever being pregnant. As soon as she had started to show, they'd kept her off school and put it down to an ongoing illness, and they'd kept her away from anybody in their small community; they couldn't bear the stigma of their so-called respectable family name and prefect daughter being labelled a 'Jezebel!' That was the turn of phrase they used every time the subject came up in the family home when Shelley dared to raise the possibility of keeping the child.

Coming back to her senses, Shelley had to watch as the man proceeded to take her precious son out of his crib, awakening him in the process. He took the baby out of the room and out of her life forever, but not before she got one long last look at him, his baby-blue eyes burning an everlasting image into her memory.

All she could do was whisper, 'I'm so sorry,' and watch as her perfect little bundle was carried away, through the door, and down the long corridor until she could no longer catch sight of him.

'It's for the best, dear, you'll realise soon enough,' her mother said.

Shelley had no reply.

'Right, no point in hanging around here now,' her father said coldly. 'Get your things, we're going home!'

***

The unnamed boy spent the next few weeks in a short-term foster placement in Kendal, before finally being adopted by the McMullens. He quickly settled into his new home on Whitehaven's Cumbrian coastline with his ecstatic new parents, William and Victoria — or Billy and Vicky as they were more commonly known.

Billy was a fisherman, who worked at sea six days a week to put food on the table and provide for him and his wife. He had been a fisherman ever since leaving school at sixteen without qualifications; he'd always wanted to follow in his father's footsteps and knew he would end up working on the fishing boats after school, so never really applied himself academically. He was content with his lot in life — having a child was just the icing on the cake for him, as he was well aware it had always been Vicky's dream to be a mother, ever since they had got together at a local dance when they were both in their late teens. It was hard to think that the dance was nearly twenty years ago.

Vicky worked part-time at the local grocery shop, until she gave it up to spend time raising their new son. Other than being a wife and a mother, she didn't harbour any secret ambitions; she was just content at having a loving, faithful husband and nice home together. She was overcome with joy upon receiving the news that their application for adoption had been approved and couldn't wait to finally be a complete family and experience the joy that motherhood brings.

And so, the McMullens took Jonathon in and raised him as though he was their own flesh and blood. The young boy couldn't have hoped for a more doting, committed, loving family. They showered him with affection and proudly showed him off everywhere that they went, always referring to him when asked as their precious little miracle. By the time Jonathon was eighteen months old, all thoughts of adoption were distant memories, as Jonathon was now very much a McMullen, and an integral part of the family. They had witnessed him grow from a baby, crawling, learning to walk and hearing him utter his first words of 'dada', into the toddler before them.

Young Jonathon was an extremely happy child. He was very inquisitive and interactive with anybody he came into contact with, always smiling and laughing and very much at home with the only parents he had ever known. At three years old his parents placed him in a local nursery, and all the workers there would often say to Vicky when she came to collect him just how adorable he was and how much he lit up the room with his gentle nature and love of cuddles. By the age of five he was attending Whitehaven Primary School and had developed a love of rugby and fishing, as usually Billy would take him to one or the other for some father-son bonding time every

Sunday on his only day off. Young Jonathon would look forwards to this each weekend, as he missed his father during the week and would sometimes stand for ages staring out of the window just waiting for his daddy to return from sea. It was around this time that the couple decided to get Jonathon a puppy for Christmas; the couple thought it was hilarious that every time an animal programme came on TV, Jonathon would stop whatever it was he was doing and just sit intently, eyes fixed firmly on the screen as though it cast an unbreakable spell over the usually hyperactive boy they knew and loved.

The couple couldn't wait to see the look on Jonathon's face when he woke that Christmas morning. Indeed, they didn't have to wait long as he was up at five in the morning, eager to open all the presents laid out nicely under the tree for him. It wasn't until he had stopped ripping the paper off the presents that he noticed a strange sound coming from the kitchen. Still in his pyjamas, he ran through to the kitchen to investigate.

In front of him was a large square object that was loosely covered in wrapping paper. He turned to his parents next to him for approval, before removing the paper in one swift swipe, revealing a metal crate containing the twelve-week-old springer spaniel his parents had bought for him. Jonathon's face spoke a thousand words as he held back tears of joy, and could barely contain his excitement. He turned to his parents and threw his arms around them then quickly turned back around to see the wagging tail of the tiny jet black puppy looking straight up at him.

'This is for you, son', his father said to him. 'He was lonely and wanted a best friend to play with, and we thought that could be you. What do you think?'

The only words Jonathon could get out were, 'Thanks, Daddy. I love him.'

The parents looked at each other and smiled before asking Jonathon to name him. He answered without a second thought.

'Toby.'

'Toby it is, then.'

Jonathon spent the remainder of the day playing with his new best friend, finally falling asleep cuddling Toby on the couch after his perfect Christmas day.

Unbeknown to the family, that day was to be their last proper Christmas together, as in the spring of the following year Vicky was diagnosed with pancreatic cancer. After months of chemotherapy they were delivered the devastating news in October of that year, that because the type of cancer was so aggressive, unfortunately the tumour had spread; it was terminal and she only had possibly three months left to live.

This absolutely broke the couple's hearts; after spending years trying to get what they had now, the sad realisation set in that it was all going to be taken away from them so suddenly and abruptly. Vicky was distraught at the fact she would never get to see her son grow into a man, and that she would miss out on all the important events in his life. She had but one last request to ask her husband, and that request was given to him from her hospice bed in late November when she made Billy promise to make sure Jonathon was taken care of, and to cherish him and give him the upbringing and love she could not now provide. She then reminded Billy not to forget her, and always remember how much she loved him and Jonathon. A tear-soaked Billy vowed to keep his promise whilst holding her hand as she laid in her bed, knowing it was just a matter of time before her now weak and fragile body could fight no longer. That cruel twist of fate came just two weeks before Christmas, when Vicky's heavily morphine-sedated body finally gave up its fight. All Billy could do was sit and watch as his beloved wife drew her last breath and eventually passed away. The heartbroken Billy gave his wife a long, lingering kiss on her forehead, told her he would always love her, and said goodbye as the doctor pronounced that she was finally at peace and free from her suffering.

***

All Billy could think of now was how to explain to his son that mummy would never be coming home. He did so by telling him that the angels needed help in heaven and that they had taken her to be one of them, then reassured him that she would always be looking over him. Jonathon didn't really understand, he just knew that his daddy was very upset and wasn't himself. Billy just wrapped his arms around his boy, and cuddled him tighter than he ever had before and told him it was just the two of them now and that he would always be there for him. At the time he said it, he meant it with genuine sincerity.

That Christmas, Billy did all he could do to ensure Jonathon had a great time, but it just didn't feel the same without his wife and he was really struggling to hold it all together. Over the following weeks he really started to go downhill rapidly. He became dishevelled, he wasn't going to work, and he was hitting the bottle hard. Jonathon's schooling and wellbeing started to suffer because of it, and many a morning he would come downstairs and attempt to rouse his father from a drunken slumber lying on the couch, to no avail. This continued for a couple of months, and as Billy's depression became deeper and deeper, his alcohol consumption grew and grew.

Jonathon's teachers became very concerned for his wellbeing after noticing a massive decline in his appearance over the past few months, and after bringing Mr McMullen in for a meeting to voice their concerns, Billy broke down and admitted that he was in a dark place and felt unable to cope, and that he needed help with Jonathon. He even admitted to the head teacher how he had contemplated suicide on several occasions lately. This immediately set alarm bells ringing, and the head informed Social Services of his disclosure, and once again the local authorities were back in the young boy's life, at first offering respite days, which steadily turned into full weekends as the depths of Billy's depression grew deeper and deeper. By now, Billy's alcoholism was out of control and he was frequently becoming involved in bar brawls and being picked up by the police on other alcohol-related offences.

Finally in May 1979, just three months before his seventh birthday, Jonathon was once again placed in the care of Social Services. Billy did try to stop it from happening, but as much as he loved his son, he just couldn't recover from the loss of his wife and reluctantly accepted that being with him was not the best place for Jonathon. This was a double blow for Billy as not only did he lose the son him and his wife desperately strived for, but he knew with it he had broken the one last promise he had vowed to his dying wife. The guilt eventually proved to be too much for Billy to take. One lonely, drink-filled night, whilst clutching a picture of the three of them in happier times, he swallowed two full packets of sleeping pills and another couple of packets of paracetamol he found lying around, washed them down with a litre bottle of rum, and went to sleep. It was a sleep he would never wake up from.

Chapter 6

The next few weeks and months seemed to pass by in a haze for Jonathon as he moved from one short term foster placement to another. His young mind struggled to comprehend the loss of his mother and father. He tried his best to pretend it hadn't really happened, and would often say his parents were away on holiday and would be coming to collect him as soon as they returned. When challenged on this by any of the foster parents, Jonathon would become extremely aggressive, and would frequently lash out at anybody that dared to question what he was saying. He felt lost and alone, not knowing where he was going to end up next. With nobody to save him from the hurt he was feeling, he shut himself off from everyone around him and became very insular, refusing to engage with anybody. Any attempts by Social workers, foster parents or child psychologists to get him to open up were met with conflict and extremely challenging behaviour, which meant it became very difficult to find Jonathon any new adoptive parents willing to take him in.

It wasn't until just after Jonathon's eighth birthday, after spending the last fifteen months moving from one failed placement to another, that Jonathon was given the news that he was to be placed with well-established and recognised long-term foster carers: James and Edna Beattie. Apart from his obvious apprehension, he was quite excited when he was told he would be living on a cattle farm in a small town named Silloth on the Solway coastline, and that Mr Beattie was an animal lover who always had a dog on the farm. This was the main selling point for Jonathon, as not only did he miss his parents, he would often wonder how Toby was and who he was living with these days. He longed to fill the void left by Toby, so agreed to go and meet the Beatties.

***

As Jonathon and his Social worker pulled up at the Beatties' farm, they were greeted at the front gate by a slightly rotund, red-faced, blond man in denim jeans, a checked shirt and wellington boots who introduced himself.

'Hi. Name's James Beattie, but friends call me Jim, or Jimmy'.

By his side was a small, thin, dark haired lady who was still wearing a blue and white striped pinafore, who explained how she had just finished preparing a lovely thick-crust steak pie and had just placed it in the oven awaiting Jonathon's arrival. Jonathon was pleased to see the Beatties' obedient black and white sheepdog, Amber, sat at James' feet.

'So, young man, you must be Jonathon?' said Mr Beattie.

Jonathon had been in this situation quite a number of times over the past year upon meeting potential foster parents. He never usually responded, as he knew it would only be a matter of time before he would be rejected once again, so didn't normally try to form a bond with anyone. However, something felt different this time and, for the first time in longer than he could care to remember, he actually responded to Mr Beattie.

'Yes sir.'

'Oh don't be nervous, Jonathon. We don't bite around here, lad, and please, just call me Jim.'

Jonathon, feeling a little less anxious by this point, and still struggling to focus on anything other than

Amber sat by her master's feet, just replied, 'Ok, Jim'.

With introductions now out of the way, the Beatties set about making Jonathon relaxed in this new, unfamiliar environment.

'Edna, why don't you show the boy around the house and where he is going to be staying. In fact, take Amber whilst you are at it, as I've heard that Jonathon is a dog lover like myself. Let him get used to the old girl whilst me and Brian have a little chat.'

Brian, Jonathon's Social worker, had been a friend of Jim for many years.

'No problem, dear,' Edna responded, before ushering Jonathon down the path and into the farmhouse with Amber padding along beside them.

After about thirty minutes of looking around the farmhouse and surrounding buildings and cattle sheds, Jonathon actually started to quite like the place, and started to imagine what it was going to be like living there. The Beatties sure seemed like decent enough people — very friendly and welcoming. He liked the idea of running around and playing in the fields with Amber, and he was also intrigued by all the cattle on the farm and the idea of managing all the animals. They went back to where Jim and Brian were still stood talking and Edna informed them that dinner was ready. Then they all headed into the house to sit and eat the steak pie she had prepared especially for them.

'So, Jonathon, what do you think of Mr and Mrs Beatties' farm then, is it somewhere you could see yourself living?' asked Brian, as they all sat about the dining table. With a rare smile, Jonathon just nodded his head; he was too busy devouring the lovely home cooked meal in front of him to notice as the adults exchanged looks as if to say, 'Everything will be just fine'.

After they had all finished their meals, Brian and Jonathon thanked the Beatties for their hospitality and said their goodbyes.

'I assure you both, the pleasure was all ours, and we can't wait to see you back here soon, Jonathon,' Mr Beattie said, as they made their way out of the door and towards the parked car at the end of the lane.

'See, Jonathon, that wasn't so bad was it?' Brian asked, as they got into the car.

Jonathon, bursting with newfound excitement, decided to engage with Brian for the first time in months, as normally he blamed Brian for all the upheaval and failed placements he has been through. Wide-eyed, sensing his life was about to change for the better, he finally dropped his guard.

'I can't wait, it's going to be great being so close to all those animals every day.'

'And what about the Beatties?' Brian then asked him.

'Oh, they seem pretty cool, too,' came his reply, as they made their way out of the farm and away from the Beattie household.

A week later, Jonathon moved into his new home with the Beatties and totally threw himself into farm living. He wanted to know all about the cows, sheep and goats that they kept, and would follow Jim everywhere asking question after question. He quickly settled into the responsibilities that came with looking after so many animals, and soon learnt how everything worked. He would help Jim to milk the cows every day, and the two of them started to build up what Jonathon thought to be a strong mutual friendship. For the first time since his parents had passed away, he started to accept that they were gone and he had to start a new life for himself. In that moment, he decided he was going to behave for the Beatties and try to become part of the family. Even Amber had taken a liking to him, and the two of them were becoming inseparable.

***

Jonathon was enrolled and started to attend Silloth Junior School two weeks after moving into the farm, and he soon started making new friends and learning to trust again after being let down all too often in his short life. Everything was really starting to look up for him and he was starting to enjoy life again.

Then, one night, about a month into his stay there, he was awoken around midnight by raised voices. Mr Beattie and his wife were having a heated argument in the kitchen. He could barely make out what was being said, but he could, however, sense the anger and venom in Jim's tone. He also heard Edna telling Jim to lower his voice so as not to wake Jonathon.

He was taken aback and shocked to hear Jim's reply.

'FUCK THAT LITTLE SHIT! IF HE WAKES UP I'LL PUT HIM BACK TO SLEEP, THE CHEEKY LITTLE BASTARD!'

Jonathon did not know what to make of this, as he'd thought Mr Beattie genuinely liked him. He laid there in his bed not knowing why he had angered Jim, pondering what he could have possibly done to upset him. He didn't know at this time, but Jim would sometimes go out with his friends to the local pubs and drink copious amounts of whiskey before staggering home and becoming abusive towards his wife Edna, often becoming physical towards her too. She had become accustomed to his ways and accepted it as part of her marriage to him, but all Jonathon could do was just lie there, frozen in his bed as he listened to the shouting going on downstairs from Mr Beattie, and then the inevitable sobbing and whimpering from Edna thereafter.

***

The next morning at breakfast, the first thing Jonathon noticed was the swollen cut on Edna's lip, along with the black eye she had sustained the night before at her husband's hand. Jim was nowhere to be seen, as he was still sleeping off the after effects of last night's liquor. Jonathon had never witnessed anything like this before, as he had never even heard his parents argue, let alone become violent. He wondered if he was to blame.

Edna, sensing the look of shock and fear in his face, swiftly tried to put the boy at ease, and tried to play it down by saying she had tripped on the tiled kitchen floor after mopping before bed. Jonathon knew she was lying but chose to accept her version of events so as not to rock the boat. As he left that morning for school, he once again felt isolated and alone; he had an overwhelming feeling that this was to become yet another failed placement. He still believed that it must've been his fault that Jim had struck his wife, and therefore decided he must try harder to please him so that it didn't happen again.

The couple of days that followed were very tentative for Jonathon, as he did his utmost to please Jim, trying to regain the relationship they had prior to the incident in the kitchen that night, as he really had felt a sense of belonging before that had happened and just wanted everything back the way it was. He convinced himself that it must have been a one off, while Jim just continued as though nothing had ever happened. One thing Jonathon knew in his mind though, was that he was sure he did not want to anger him; he was scared Jim might just take it out on him the next time he came home drunk and angry. Jonathon just did as much as he could to help out from that day forward, and he would sometimes spend hours after school tending to the cattle with his new best friend, Amber, by his side. He tried desperately to prove to Jim that it was worth keeping him around, but also, he didn't to be in the firing line if something was to happen.

That day didn't come until seven weeks after that

initial incident. Jonathon, by this time, had settled back into a routine, and had tried to forget about Edna's bruised and swollen features. If truth be known, he even started to question the realness of the incident in his own mind — it was as if he had dreamt it. He didn't want to have a distorted picture of Jim, the man he respected and looked up to for a giving him a home in this picturesque surrounding, the man who had taken him in and befriended him. Before that night, Jonathon had even thought of him as a father figure. Yet after that one evening, seven weeks later, the young boy's opinion of Jim was to alter forever.

Whilst lying in his bed, not quite awake, but not yet sound asleep, Jonathon was startled by raised voices again coming from downstairs, but this time there were more than just Jim and Edna's voices. He thought he could also make out the distinct West Cumbrian twang of his Social worker, Brian. This immediately got his young, curious mind thinking. Were they talking about him? Had the Beatties finally had enough of him and called in Brian to come and collect him during the night? With these thoughts of uncertainty racing through his head, he decided he would creep downstairs and listen to what was being said.

As he got to the bottom of the stairs, he was certain at this point that it was definitely Brian's voice that he could hear, but still wasn't sure at this stage of the reason for his visit. As Jonathon crept around in the hall, he was quite surprised to hear Jim and Brian casually chatting away and laughing together. Still puzzled by what was happening, he entered the kitchen under the pretence of needing a drink.

As Jonathon made his way towards the sink, he could clearly see Jim and Brian sat around the dining room table. The two men were smoking cigars, and in front of them were two glasses of whiskey; the rest of the half-empty bottle lay close by. Edna was busy attending to the laundry and preparing to iron Jonathon's school clothes for the following day.

'Hey, look who it is!' Jim said, slurring his words slightly. 'Come say hello to "Uncle Brian", son. He's come to see how you are getting on. I've told him you're doing just grand, isn't that right, Jonathon?'

All Jonathon could offer in reply was, 'Yes, everything's going really well, I like it here, Brian.' He poured himself a glass of water at the kitchen sink.

'Well then, son, come and sit with us for a while and tell Brian all about what you have been doing here.'

Jonathon's panic at the thought of being moved had now subsided as he approached the table where the two men were sat. Mr Beattie playfully ran his sweaty hand through Jonathon's hair, then picked him up and placed him on his knee. Jonathon didn't know what to say or do as Jim had never done this before, so he just went along with it to show a united front to Brian to reaffirm just how comfortable he was living on the Beatties' farm.

Edna, sensing an overwhelming familiarity in her drunken husband's behaviour, tried to coax Jonathon away from the men and back to his bedroom.

Jim just dismissed her. 'Have you not got things you need to be doing, woman?'

Edna knew by the tone of his voice not to argue, and reluctantly exited the room, a sense of foreboding of what was to come next embedded at the forefront of her mind.

'I've just been telling Brian what a good little helper you have been around here, Jonathon, and how we would be lost without you now. You have been practically running the farm single-handed lately.'

Jonathon, feeling a sense of pride and acknowledgement for his efforts over the past few weeks, started to relax and relay to Brian all the things he had been occupying his time with, his mouth spewing out words before his mind could process them. Everything was going well until Jonathon accidentally told Brian about the incident with Jim and his wife seven weeks earlier.

Jonathon knew just how much of a mistake he had made as soon as the words had left his mouth, but it was too late, the damage had already been done: he had broken Jim's trust. He knew he should have kept his mouth shut. As Jonathon dropped his head and looked at the floor, he failed to notice as Brian winked at Jim.

'Is this true Jim?' said Brian in mock-concern. He knew exactly how Jim was towards his wife, but he was of the same ilk as Jim and believed that women should be seen and not heard, and would also sometimes 'discipline' his own wife if she dared to 'step out of line.'

'Of course it's not true, Brian,' Jim responded. 'That boy has got one vivid imagination, I tell you.' He pushed Jonathon off his lap and ordered him to go to bed. 'I will deal with you later!'

'See Jonathon, if Mr Beattie here says it didn't happen, then I believe him that it did not happen. And another thing, young man, you shouldn't go around making accusations that aren't true, especially against honest, hard-working people that were kind enough to give you a home. Now do as Jim says and get to your room!'

As Jonathon made his way out of the kitchen and through the hall, he could clearly make out Brian's words to Jim.

'Make sure you keep that boy disciplined, Jim, he can be a cheeky little shit at times. Don't give him an inch as he will try and take the piss if you let him!'

'Oh don't you worry, mate, he will get what's coming to him later, you mark my words!' Jim replied.

'Good, good, Jimmy boy, I'm just forewarning you as I've seen exactly what he can be like at previous placements, and I can assure you that that boy needs a firm hand.'

'And it's a firm hand he will get, believe me!'

Jonathon, after overhearing this, quickly ran to his room, jumped back into bed and covered himself with his duvet, hoping on the off-chance that Jim wasn't actually serious about what he had just said. He thought that if he tried to get to sleep Jim might just leave him alone. This wasn't to be the case however. As Jonathon lay there for what seemed like a decade, too afraid to go to sleep, he heard Jim see Brian out of the door and exchange goodbyes. Sheer panic set in to Jonathon's now trembling body as he heard the loud thuds of Jim's size ten boots coming ever closer up the stairs towards his bedroom. His panic soon became a reality as he watched as the handle turned. The door was flung open and he could see Jim's large frame silhouetted in the doorway.

'RIGHT YOU BIG MOUTHED LITTLE BASTARD, I'LL TEACH YOU TO KEEP YOUR TRAP SHUT!'

Jonathon watched as Jim removed his solid, brass buckled belt before dragging him from his bed by his hair, then forcefully pulling down Jonathon's pyjama bottoms and then proceeding to deliver lash after lash of the thick leather belt hard over his backside and tops of legs. The young boy screamed out for help in pain and distress, but as the farm covered many acres there was nobody to hear his screams. Nobody, of course, except Edna, who by this time was on tenterhooks on their sofa, cringing with every blow she heard. She hated herself for being too weak to intervene; instead she prayed for Jim to leave the boy alone.

Eventually Jonathon's young body could take no more, and he went limp in Jim's hands as he passed out through shock and pain and fell to the floor, laying there in a bloody heap.

Jim finally gave up and casually rethreaded his belt, straightened his hair, then made his way out of the bedroom and into the bathroom to get cleaned up before taking himself off to bed. Edna waited and waited until she was certain her husband was sleeping; she knew she was safe when she heard Jim snoring. She was shocked and horrified as she entered Jonathon's room to find him still passed out on the carpet, his body a cold mess, with blood seeping from his fresh, open wounds.

She rushed to get her first aid kit and a warm, wet flannel from downstairs, then gently dabbed the sores and bandaged him up where he lay as he slowly regained his senses. She helped place the terrified boy back into his bed and tucked him in before giving him a kiss on his forehead and instructing him to try and get some rest. As Edna quietly crept out of the room, closing the door behind her, Jonathon just lay there, dumbfounded at what had just happened. He was still reeling from the excruciating pain radiating from his backside, sobbing and too afraid to move in the dark room. He prayed for someone to come and take him from this nightmare, and started to reminisce about his mum and dad. Oh, how he wished they was still alive and everything could go back to the way it once was!

***

This was to be the turning point in Jim and Jonathon's relationship. From then on, Jim would treat Jonathon with pure contempt. Jonathon never did make it to school that next morning, as he could barely walk after the beating he had undertaken. Edna informed the school that he was unwell, and he had to stay home for the following week so nobody would be alerted to what had happened to him. This incident set a precedent for the following months, and Jim would regularly beat and take out his frustrations on Jonathon every time he was intoxicated and stressed. The beatings became more and more vicious each time. Jim was even going as far as burning the boy all over his body with cigarettes, then urinating on the wounds. Every single time, Edna would fix Jonathon up and try and make excuses for her husband. As a result, the Beatties' marriage became very strained, and any rare intimacy they shared was one sided and forced by Jim.

As the following summer approached, Jonathon could not wait for the long break; due to his troubled home life, he had again become very reserved and withdrawn. Any friends he had made previously he had since lost, as he felt as though he couldn't trust anyone — especially not his Social worker, who'd totally dismissed what he had told him that night. He also started to become a victim of bullying in school, as the other children classed him as a 'weirdo' and would often taunt him at break times. There seemed to be no respite for Jonathon, and the only thing he actually took comfort in was his one true friend, Amber, who he could often offload his problems onto. He couldn't wait for a break from it all.

Unfortunately for him, that respite did not come, as when the school term finished, the beatings became more frequent, as Jim had turned his once a week drinking sessions into full weekend events, with more and more of Jim's 'friends' attending the farm. With Jonathon being off school, Jim didn't have to worry about the teachers or other parents witnessing the horrific injuries the boy was sustaining for a while. Brian would sometimes appear from time to time, but whenever he would catch Jonathon's gaze, he would just offer him a half-arsed smirk, as if to say, 'Know your place, boy!'

***

One August summer night, just six days before Jonathon's ninth birthday, things went from bad to worse. A drunken Jim crept into Jonathon's bedroom whilst his friends continued to drink downstairs; Edna had already taken herself off to bed, as she had had just about enough of Jim and his friends. What came next for the innocent eight year old little boy still haunted him in later life.

Jim quietly woke him from his sleep by pressing his wandering hand down on the boy's leg. As Jonathon opened his eyes and looked up, he could clearly see Jim sat on the bed beside him. With one hand still on Jonathon's leg, he raised his other hand towards his face and placed his finger over his mouth as if to say, 'Be quiet'.

Once Jonathon was fully awake, he not only noticed that his bedroom door was shut, but he had to watch as Jim started to undo his trousers. Jonathon didn't have a clue what was happening, and prayed he was going to wake up and realise it was all just a bad dream. Unfortunately for him it wasn't. Totally numb, Jonathon listened as Jim whispered threateningly at him in the dark.

'Do exactly as I tell you, boy. If you tell anybody about tonight, nobody would believe you and you'll get into huge trouble for telling lies.'

Without further warning, Jim removed his penis from inside his underwear and forced Jonathon to perform fellatio on him.

'If you try anything like biting me or screaming, I promise I'll break your skinny, worthless neck and bury you in the garden.' Jim's words made Jonathon's blood run cold.

As Jonathon did as he was told, he felt sick to the pit of his stomach and could not wait for this ordeal to be over. All he could smell was the pungent, stale sweat from Jim's genitals, along with the combination of whiskey and cigar smoke that clung to him. His mouth tasted as though someone had urinated into it. Jonathon died a little bit inside that night, as he was hoping that one of the many voices he could hear coming from downstairs would come and rescue him, but it wasn't to be — he realised he was alone, nobody was coming to his aid. He had to endure this abomination of trust until Jim had finally 'relieved' himself into his mouth.

Jonathon just lay there, once again frozen in his bed, scared to move in case Jim decided to give him another beating for good measure. He managed to contain his emotions as he waited for Jim to leave the room and go back downstairs and continue drinking with his friends, as he didn't want to show Jim just exactly how petrified and upset he was. When he finally plucked up the courage to move, he ran to the bathroom to wash the vile taste from his mouth, then brushed his teeth for a good ten minutes and drank several glasses of water, but nothing could take away the feelings of shame and disgust that he was feeling.

Chapter 7

This cycle of sexual abuse and violence continued throughout the next couple of years of Jonathon's life, but by now other men were starting to become involved too. Unbeknown to Jonathon, Jim and his so-called 'friends' from the lodge, were actually part of a secret paedophile ring that spanned throughout Cumbria. Many of them took in children in care, often referred to them by the Social worker, Brian Jenkins — the same man that just happened to be Jonathon's Social worker. Quite a number of them had high-profile jobs in authority, which made a perfect cover for their more deviant indulgencies.

Jonathon was now twelve years old and had become quite desensitised to the abuse bestowed upon him. He would often lock himself away in his room for hours watching action movies on the VHS recorder he had received from the Beatties for Christmas. His favourite actors were Charles Bronson and Bruce Lee, as he loved how masculine and tough they were. He would sit and watch their movies over and over and dream of one day becoming like them. He knew they wouldn't be the type of people to let others abuse them the way he had been abused, and he was in awe of their strength and courage.

It was also around this time that he picked up and started to read the Bible that had been in his bedside drawer ever since he arrived at the farm.

It was on one of these occasions, whilst scanning through Genesis 6:5-8 in the King James Version of the Bible, that he came across a passage he associated with.

And God saw that the wickedness of man was great in the earth, and that every imagination of the thoughts of his heart was evil continually. And it repented the Lord that he had made man on the earth, and it grieved him at his heart. And the Lord said, 'I will destroy man whom I have created from the face of the earth; both man, and beast, and the fowls of the air; for it repenteth me that I have made them'. But Noah found grace in the eyes of the Lord.

It was after reading this that Jonathon started to find solace in the Bible. Although he didn't quite understand it fully, he saw himself as Noah, and his abusers as the wicked men that God would wipe out. The thought pleased Jonathon. Thus, his interest in Christianity was born.

Jonathon actually started to look forward to and embrace his once hated Sunday morning visit to church with the Beatties, and he would take the Bible text as literal and set about studying it in its entirety for passages he could relate to and take meaning from that would offer him some form of comfort in what he was enduring.

However, there was just one thing he could not quite get his head around: if Jim was a Christian, how could he commit such devious and wicked crimes against fellow mankind?

He read a passage in Levictus 20:13 which both pleased, yet frightened him.

If a man also lie with mankind, as he lieth with a woman, both of them have committed an abomination: they shall surely be put to death; their blood shall be upon them.

For obvious reasons, he liked the idea of his abusers being put to their deaths, but he couldn't work out if this also applied to himself. He liked to think that due to him being an unwilling participant in the abuse, the Lord would give him mercy.

***

As Jonathon grew into adolescence over the following couple of years and his body matured, he started to stand up for himself a lot more, unwilling to suffer any more abuse either at home or in school. He started fighting back, and the Beatties would often get phone calls from the school to come and collect him after he had been involved in one fight or another. Even Jim, who had totally overpowered and dominated him over the past seven years, was starting to become wary of the ever growing young man before him.

Finally, the abuse came to an end after one drunken night when Jim staggered back into the farm after a heavy drinking session with his pals. He immediately started to become aggressive towards Edna for no other reason than because he could. Jonathon had then reached breaking point, and as Jim raised his hand towards his fearful wife, he received the shock of his life as the fifteen-year-old Jonathon jumped up from where he had been sitting to protect her.

'And what the fuck do you think you're doing, you ungrateful bastard?' Jim slurred. Before Jonathon could respond Jim continued. 'You're a worthless, pathetic excuse for a human being! No wonder your whore of a mother didn't want you!'

Jonathon, confused by Jim's words, retorted, 'My mum died, you fucking arsehole!'

Edna tried to intervene and retract Jim's words on his behalf, knowing what he was about to blurt out next. She tried to tell Jonathon to ignore his ramblings, and pass it off as drunken confusion, but Jim was having none of it.

'Tell the fucker, Edna, tell him how his whore of

a mother abandoned him because she didn't want the worthless bastard either! It's about time he knew anyway.'

Edna was beside herself with fury. She turned to him and, for the first time since Jonathon had been there, Edna stood up to her husband.

'THAT'S ENOUGH JIM, SHUT YOUR BIG MOUTH AND LEAVE THE BOY ALONE!'

It was too late though: the seed of madness had been planted.

Jonathon looked straight at Edna and asked her, 'What the fuck is he talking about?'

Jim interjected before Edna had the chance to speak.

'Fuck it, I'll tell you! The McMullens weren't you're real parents. Your real mother was a good for nothing whore of a schoolgirl who gave you away at birth. I should know, I've seen all your files!'

'Is this true?' Jonathon demanded of Edna.

'I'm afraid it is Jonathon — well the part about your real mother giving you up for adoption at birth anyway. I'm sorry you had to find out this way.'

Jonathon was in utter shock at this news, and could not process what he was being told. His whole life had been a lie.

'I fucking told you!' Jim sneered.

By this point Jonathon had had just about enough of listening to anything Jim had to say. Before he could spew more nasty words, Jonathon snapped and rushed towards where the drunken Jim was standing.

'I FUCKING HATE YOU!' he screamed in his face.

Then, with all the strength he could muster, Jonathon unleashed a vicious combination of punches and kicks he had secretly been practicing in his room. He delivered blow after blow to the already unsteady Jim, until he finally toppled him in a heap on the dining room floor.

Edna just stood there and watched with a hint of

a smile on her face as her bully of a husband finally received his comeuppance at the hands of the child she couldn't protect. She knew in that instance that this would be Jonathon's final night in the household, but she was happy. Happy because she knew that with it, the young man's suffering at her husband's hand had finally came to an end.

Once Jim had picked himself up off the floor, embarrassed and bloodied, he immediately pushed past his wife and went to the phone in the hall. He was initially going to call the police, but stopped himself — he was unsure what Jonathon might say to them. Instead, he called Brian and proceeded to tell him how Jonathon had beaten him in an unprovoked attack. He stated that he wanted him out of his house and out of their lives forever, and told Brian that he had until the morning to come and collect him, as he would not be welcome for more than one more night under his roof.

This came as no surprise to Jonathon, who was already by this point packing his belongings up in his room. Edna went and spoke to Jonathon whilst Jim poured himself another drink and sat brooding in silence on the sofa. He knew his hold over Jonathon was finished forever, and he had no further use for him. A tearful Edna went and sat on Jonathon's bed as he gathered all his things into his bags.

'I am so sorry Jonathon. Please forgive me for everything. I sincerely wish I could take away all the hurt and suffering you have had to go through, I really do. I'm so sorry I couldn't have stopped it, please believe me.'

Jonathon pitied Edna. He knew he had finally broken free, but he knew that she would never be strong enough to leave.

He gave her a great big hug and kissed her on the cheek. 'It's not your fault.'

Edna could barely look him in the eye due to the guilt she felt as she made her way out of his room.

'I wish you all the best for the future Jonathon, I really do. Go and find the happiness we couldn't give you.'

Those were her final words to Jonathon, as she never did see him again; she couldn't bear to look him in the face or say goodbye the following morning. Jonathon never slept a wink that night as he waited for Brian to come and collect him. He had far too many thoughts running through his mind after what he had just discovered. He also had many, many questions he needed answered from Brian too.

As Brian pulled in the long driveway leading to the farm the next morning, Jonathon went over to where the now very old and weary Amber lay in her bed. He looked deep into her eyes; as he did so, a tear fell from his eye and rolled down his cheek. He stroked his companion one last time and told her how much she had comforted him over the years, and just how much she meant to him and that he would never forget her. He gave Amber one final hug and kiss goodbye, then grabbed his bags and made his way outside, straight into Brian's waiting car without looking back.

'Are... are you okay?' Brian asked hesitantly.

Jonathon gave him a cold look. 'Get me away from this fucking place, NOW!'

Brian was not accustomed to this new found attitude and foul language coming from Jonathon. Wary after receiving Jim's call the previous night stating how Jonathon had allegedly battered him in an unprovoked attack, Brian decided not to delve any deeper — he did not want to be on the receiving end of Jonathon's wrath. Instead, he did as Jonathon had asked and left the farm without even speaking to Jim or Edna.

'So, Brian, why didn't you tell me I was adopted, and that my real mother gave me away at birth?' Jonathon asked a now uptight Brian.

'Err, well, the thing is Jonathon, with you being under sixteen, and still classed as a minor in the eyes of the law, we as Social workers have a duty of care to provide to you. We do what we think is in your best interests. Besides, we can't legally give you this information until you turn sixteen, when it is deemed you are old enough to be able to understand and cope with this information.' Seeing the look on Jonathon's face, he continued hurriedly, 'But seeing as you are coming up sixteen in a few short months, what do you want to know?'

'I want to know everything,' Jonathon replied. 'Who am I? Where am I from? But first of all you can start off by telling me who my mother is. My real mother!'

'I don't really know much about her to be honest Jonathon, as I was only assigned as your Social worker after you had been placed with the McMullen's. All I know is her name, which is, or was, Shelley Winter.'

'And what about my real father?'

'He was never named on your birth certificate, so I'm afraid I honestly can't help you on that one.'

Jonathon just sat there, processing this information. Why had his mother left him? Who was she as a person? What was so bad about him that she had to give him up?

At this moment he thought of another passage from his Bible, which he was now becoming more and more familiar with. He remembered Isaiah 49:15.

Can a woman forget her sucking child, that she should not have compassion on the son of her womb? Yea, they may forget, yet I will not forget thee.

Jonathon just sat there quietly for the rest of the journey, running this verse over and over in his head, each time emphasising the last sentence: he would not be forgotten.

He spent the next couple of months in a residential care home in Workington, Cumbria, with four other young people from different areas. He never really spoke more than two words to any of them.

The others never bothered him though, as he was now a solid-framed, stocky teenager with muscles bigger than normal for someone of his age; the last few years of lifting hay bales and helping out around the farm obviously had some benefits. That, along with his piercing blue eyes and rugged features, meant that the other kids were quite wary of him. His brooding, introverted nature just added to his enigma, so the others gave Jonathon a very wide berth during his time in the home.

***

Jonathon turned sixteen in the August of 1989, and as the local authorities no longer had a legal responsibility over him, they helped him get his own flat, sorted out his benefits, and sent him on his way, not before giving him the only information they had regarding his mother, which was his birth certificate, and his chronology from the day he was born and all throughout the course of his time in care. Jonathon by now just wanted to get as far away from there as possible. He wanted to forget his past. The more he thought about trying to track down his mother, the more he despised her for leaving him to endure the agonising traumas of his short life. As far as he was concerned, the McMullen's were, and would always, be his true parents. Within the first few weeks of living on his own, in an attempt to bury everything about his past, he immediately changed his name via Deed Poll, opting to amalgamate his two heroes Charles Bronson, and Bruce Lee, giving him his new title, Charles Lee. He secretly hoped he could emulate their bravery, and felt as though this would be the start of his metamorphosis from victim to hero; and with it, he decided to enlist into the Army, specifically the King's Own Royal Border Regiment, (KORBR).

Chapter 8

After passing his initial army fitness and aptitude tests with flying colours, Charles, to give him his new title, was accepted and enlisted into this proud regiment. Due to his high entry-level score, he had numerous options to choose from rather than just infantry fodder. He decided he wanted to become a medic, as he quite liked the idea of patching up wounded soldiers; it kind of reminded him of the times Edna had bathed and bandaged up his wounds. He was still so grateful that she at least offered some form of comfort in extremely difficult times. He genuinely wanted to do the same for others. He just needed to get through the twenty-four weeks of basic training at Catterick Garrison first, before he could then go on to do a further twenty-four weeks of training to become a Combat Medical Technician.

Charles, strangely, settled in with relative ease and discovered a new found purpose in his life. He loved the sense of unity and camaraderie that it brought him. He even made a few friends along the way — though he never allowed himself to become too close to anyone. The one thing that Charles really loved, though, was the sense of strength and power he was starting to feel. Whenever his fellow recruits would get down time, Charles would often be found honing his physique in the barracks' gym, determined never again to be in a position where he found himself overpowered and at somebody else's mercy.

With sheer determination and goal-orientated ambition, Charles made light work of his initial basic training, and was so proud when he and his group of new recruits received their passing out parade at twenty-four weeks.

However, when everybody else was heading home for two weeks leave, Charles had nowhere to go; he had already given up his flat — he never wanted to return to the area that held so many bad memories for him. He instead chose to stay at the barracks and throw himself into more training, something which didn't go unnoticed by his commanding officer Marcus Lancaster. Funnily enough, Marcus was also actually from Lancaster, and it was well known throughout the unit that his family had held a long tradition of serving in the (KORBR) and that he was from a very well-respected family. This would explain how, at only twenty-one years of age, he was already a well-respected officer in the regiment.

'Quite the dedicated soldier aren't you, Charlie boy?' Marcus remarked as Charles was delivering blow after blow to the heavy bag that hung from the gym wall.

'I try my best sir. Don't you encourage us to "be all that we can be"?'

Marcus chuckled. 'You're absolutely correct, Charlie, indeed we do. I see you are hitting that bag with real bad intentions. Have you had any form of boxing training in the past?'

He watched with interest as Charles wiped the sweat from his face at the end of yet another round.

'No, sir, I just enjoy channelling my aggression through the bag, sir. It helps me to relax.'

'I know exactly what you mean, Charlie,' came Marcus' reply. 'What say you and me get in the ring and I'll teach you a few moves? We could use someone like you in our boxing team — what do you reckon?'

Charles, not quite sure what he meant by 'someone like you', didn't want to cause offence, so he just agreed and climbed through the ropes into the ring with Marcus. The older man found a real respect for the younger as he put him through his paces, thinking he would soon start to tire as he shouted out command after command. It wasn't to be, as Charles thrived between the ropes and relentlessly delivered combinations as instructed by Marcus.

After a gruelling ten three-minute rounds, on top of the bag work he had already put in, Charles seemed somewhat raring to continue, whereas Marcus was ready for a breather.

'How about we call it a day for now, Charlie, eh? We don't want to be burning you out lad.'

He'd enjoyed the workout with Charles though, and the one thing he really took from it was just how much potential he had seen in the young man. He slapped Charles on the back.

'I would really like you to come and try out for the team when the company returns, Charlie, I think you would be a great asset. Do you think that would be something you would be interested in?'

Charles was not used to this kind of praise. 'Yes sir, I think I'll give it a go,' he said, shocked.

'Well don't think too hard, Charlie, I could really do with you on the team. It's about time we beat them navy bastards!'

It only just dawned on Charles now that this wasn't any old training session. Marcus had actually been watching him with clear interest over the past few weeks and, with the upcoming Inter Service boxing tournament only six weeks away, Marcus had hoped that the promising young fighter would throw his name into the hat. But without that happening until now, he had decided to take matters into his own hands. Therefore it had been no coincidence he had met Charles in the gym that day.

Charles threw himself into his Combat Medical Technician training over the following weeks. He did, however, take Marcus up on his offer, and after impressing the army boxing coach, he excitedly joined the team and was matched up to fight another young heavyweight from the Royal Navy's boxing team at the upcoming tournament.

***

For the next three weeks he underwent some seriously intensive sparring sessions with the other fighters, and when fight night finally arrived, he was raring to get through the ropes and unleash his inner fury on to his opponent. His opponent was a big, bulky, young black male from London's tough east end, by the name of Tyrone Williams. After knocking out his last two opponents, Tyrone was highly confident and had huge expectations from his fellow team members and coach, especially when they learnt that he was up against a novice in his first bout. This did not faze Charles, however, as he knew he was accustomed to receiving heavy beatings over the years. If he could take the pain Jim had put him through all those years and not be broken, there was no way anyone was going to beat him in the ring!

As the bell sounded at the beginning of the first round, Tyrone rushed menacingly towards Charles, planning to bully him with his size and strength until he finally succumbed to the pressure. It was fruitless, however, as Charles had a game plan of his own — although very simplistic in nature. The plan was to just keep on hitting the larger Tyrone with every ounce of strength he could find, and not stop until one of them was either knocked out or unable to continue.

Tyrone managed to land the first couple of shots, bloodying Charles' nose in doing so, and sensed he was in for an easy win as he tried to pin Charles against the ropes and into the corner. Charles tried to remember what his coach had said to him about remaining calm under pressure and not fighting in anger, as this only caused you to make mistakes. He decided to ignore this advice though, as he could feel a burning rage deep inside of him. No longer would he stand back and be on the receiving end of violence.

In that split second he remembered all the action movies he used to watch, and thought especially about his two heroes, as Tyrone tried to land yet another combination. Time to fight back, he thought.

As Tyrone swung a big overhand punch towards his face, what happened next stunned and amazed the crowd: Charles unleashed a shuddering left hook that seemed to travel all the way from the soles of his feet, right through his body, before finally landing with devastating effect right on the side of Tyrone's jaw line.

Tyrone was instantly knocked out by the vicious blow. The crowd were in uproar; all of Charles' fellow platoon from 'S' company had gathered to watch and were absolutely blown away as the nearing seventeen-year-old underdog, Charles, totally annihilated the Navy's hot prospect inside the first round.

'That was fantastic, Charlie boy! I knew you had a natural ability for boxing, I just knew it!' Marcus babbled, as they made their way back to the communal dressing room where the other fighters awaited their bouts.

Charles wasn't used to this new found adoration and positive reinforcement, but it was welcomed nonetheless. Charles' popularity grew over the following weeks as the other recruits, many of which were a few years older than him, formed a mutual respect for their brother in arms, and any thoughts of his time at the Beatties' farm were pushed to one side as Charles now realised he was the one in control of his own life and destiny, and he relished this new found control.

***

As he approached the end of his twenty-four weeks Medical Combat Technician training, Charles watched with great interest as things were really starting to get serious in the Persian Gulf. The Iraqi Dictator, Saddam Hussein, had ordered the invasion and occupation of Kuwait, his apparent aim being the acquisition of the nation's large oil reserves and expanding Iraqi power in the region. On August 3rd 1990, the United Nations Security Council called for Iraq to withdraw from Kuwait. On the 6th of August, just five days before Charles' eighteenth birthday, the Council ordered a worldwide ban on trade with Iraq. Iraq's response was to formally annex Kuwait on the 8th of August, thus posing a potential threat to Saudi Arabia, the world's largest oil producer and exporter. This in turn prompted the United States and its Western European NATO allies to rush troops to Saudi Arabia to defer a possible attack. Egypt and several other Arab nations joined the anti-Iraq coalition and contributed forces to the military build-up, known as Operation Desert Shield. Iraq meanwhile built up its occupying army in Kuwait to about 300,000 troops.

Charles and the rest of his platoon from 'S' company were given the news on the 29th November that year, just three months since Charles' eighteenth birthday, that they were to be deployed to the Gulf with immediate effect. Saddam steadfastly refused to withdraw Iraqi forces from Kuwait, however: he maintained that it would remain a province of Iraq.

Charles, although nervous at receiving this news, secretly revelled in the prospect of entering into a live combat area and putting his new skills to the test as he and his 'brothers' prepared themselves for their forthcoming six-month tour of duty, led by his friend and mentor Marcus Lancaster. The company landed in Saudi Arabia a week later to prepare for instructions. The men received orders they were to take part in Operation Granby, the objective being to flank the opposition Iraqi forces from the left and eventually force them to withdraw from Kuwait.

***

The allied coalition's military offensive against Iraq began on January 16th – 17th 1991, with a massive U.S.-led air campaign that continued throughout the war. Over the next few weeks, this sustained aerial bombardment, which had been named Operation Desert Storm, destroyed Iraq's air defences, before attacking its communication networks, government buildings, weapons plants, oil refineries, bridges and roads. By mid-February, the allies had shifted their attacks to Iraq's forward ground forces in Kuwait and southern Iraq, destroying their fortifications and tanks.

This gave way to Operation Desert Sabre, a massive allied ground offensive, which was launched northward from eastern Saudi Arabia into Kuwait and southern Iraq on February 24th. Within three days, Arab and U.S forces had retaken Kuwait city in the face of crumbling Iraqi resistance, assisted by the British-led coalition forces from the west — including 'S' company from the King's Own Royal Border Regiment. During this short period, Charles and his unit encountered many pockets of Iraq's elite Republican Guard units, as they side swiped them from the left. The Republican Guard was a fierce and well-respected foe, and Marcus' men found themselves coming under heavy enemy fire on numerous occasions. It was on one of these occasions in particular, whilst trying to force the enemy to retreat, that 'S' company endured their first and only fatality. One that would prove to have a massive impact on Charles' life.

Whilst engaged in live combat with the enemy, and sustaining round after round of Kalashnikov AK 47 gunfire just outside of Kuwait city, the men from 'S' company found themselves outnumbered and surrounded, after breaking away from the other allied forces they were recently with to go on a reconnaissance mission to gather intelligence on enemy troops' numbers and weaponry. As Marcus led the men into a desolate industrial estate just on the outskirts of the city, he inadvertently led them into an ambush; somewhere in the region of forty Republican Guards were strategically hidden in the buildings scattered around them.

As soon as the enemy spotted the company of eighteen men, they opened fire, quickly pinning 'S' company into a small, two storey building — right in the centre of their firing line.

The men's training quickly took over before panic could set in, and they took up positions inside the building, close to the broken windows and doors where they could return a volley of fire at the opposing troops.

Charles' heart felt as though it would burst right out through his chest as he composed himself and returned short bursts of fire from his standard issue SA80 assault rifle. Although the hairs on the back of his neck stood upright, he was buzzing with adrenaline. He felt as though he was John Rambo from the Sylvester Stallone movies he had seen growing up.

This went on for the next couple of hours, as Marcus called for aerial support, and was informed that all allied air forces were currently engaged in other active zones. The men just had to dig in and hope that support would come before their ammunition ran out, carefully picking off targets with single bursts as the enemy tried to close in on them. All around them, all they could hear in between grenade blasts and heavy duty rounds, were chants of, 'Allahu Akbar' — 'God is great' — as the opposing troops sensed a small victory and bayed for western blood. An overwhelming sense of inevitable doom fell upon Charles and his platoon.

'EVERYBODY TAKE COVER!'

'RPG INCOMING!'

Before any of them had time to react, the rocket propelled grenade tore right through the side of the building, totally exposing the north-westerly rooms to enemy sniper fire. The next thing Charles heard were the screams of one of his fellow soldiers as a .32 calibre sniper round tore right through his thigh muscle, dropping him instantly and leaving him vulnerable to another shot that would possibly end his life.

Charles automatically sprang into action and dragged the man out of his vulnerable exposure and pulled him into cover, away from the possible scope aimed at him. His medic training quickly coming to the forefront of his mind, he desperately checked to see if the bullet had hit the femoral artery. Fortunately for the man it hadn't, and there was no trace of left over fragment remaining in the wound as he poured his canteen over it, cleaning the charred wound and swiftly bandaging the leg to stem the blood flow. His colleagues continued to battle on and fire covering rounds to give him time to work.

Just as he finished applying the dressing, his attention was diverted as one, then another, RPG rained down on the crumbling building they were using for cover. The next wave of attack more devastating than the one before. Just as Charles managed to regain composure and offer return fire with the other men, he was blown clean off his feet as two mortar rounds hit the building simultaneously. Dazed and confused, with ringing in his ears as he struggled to stand back upright, he could make out two of his unit lying on the ground: one appeared to be unconscious, and the other was Marcus, his commanding officer.

As he neared to where Marcus was lying, he could clearly make out a great amount of blood that seemed to be coming from Marcus' abdomen. As he rushed to the officer's aid, he could make out a welcoming sound overhead. He recognised the distinct sound of the approaching Apache helicopters, and knew aerial support was close by.

'Hold on Marcus, they're here, they're coming for us.'

He quickly set about investigating the extent of Marcus' injury. By now he was able to work undisturbed as the two helicopters above made light work of the Republican Guards futile resistance, quickly eliminating the enemy before bringing the choppers down and offering ground support. Charles got the shock of his life as he removed Marcus' desert camouflage then his Kevlar body armour. He reeled as he saw a ten inch laceration just above Marcus' waist — just below where the body armour offered protection. There was a six inch piece of shrapnel sticking out from the wound, and the young officer's intestines were protruding out through the opening it had created. Marcus could see the look of fear in Charles' eyes as he desperately tried to keep the intestines from falling out even further.

Charles administered Marcus with morphine to numb the panic and pain the officer must be feeling. He tried to offer Marcus reassuring words, but knew it was in vain: there was no way he could stem the increasing blood flow, and he knew he would not make the journey back to base. Charles stopped trying to hold the torso together and chose instead to take his friend's hand in his own. He looked Marcus straight in the eye and began to cry — there was nothing more he could do for his dying friend.

'I'm sorry, Marcus. I'm so sorry, mate, there's nothing I can do. Please forgive me.'

Through a pain contorted face, Marcus looked up at Charles and told him. 'It's ok, Charlie boy, you did good today, my friend. We fought a good fight. Just do me one favour would you, please?'

'Anything, Marcus, what do you want?' Charles replied.

'Would you tell my father I tried my best to make

him proud? Tell him how well we fought today, please.'

'Of course I will, mate, no problem.'

Marcus then offered one last remark to his young friend that cut Charles deep to the bone.

'It has been a real honour fighting alongside you, Charlie boy. I couldn't have wished for a better man to watch my back.'

'The honour was all mine, sir,' Charles said, his voice choked with emotion as he sat and watched his friend's eyes close for the very last time.

Charles knelt there, tears streaking his face, for a very long time as he looked at the dead body before him. He was numb and in shock when the helicopter crew came and helped him and the other wounded men from the building, into the choppers, and away to safety.

That was the last action Charles was part of in active duty, as the U.S. President George Bush declared a cease fire on February 28th, just a day later, after the last remaining Iraqi resistance collapsed completely. The way was clear for 'S' company to return back to the U.K.

Charles tried to settle back into normal military duties upon his return to Britain, but something just didn't feel right anymore. Over the following weeks and months he reverted back to his old ways, switching himself off from the rest of the platoon, only doing the bare minimum required of him in his role. He became extremely disillusioned with military life, and felt immense grief and guilt for not being able to save his dying friend.

Nobody could quite figure out what was wrong with Charles as he became more and more introverted. Even his boxing coach could not get him back into his once ritualistic training regime. Slowly, he fell into a deep, dark depression over the following six months, to the point where he wasn't even bothering to adhere to the strict army disciplines anymore. He was spending more and more time in the military prison for insubordination as he was becoming extremely difficult to manage and very challenging of authority. It wasn't until the summer of 1992 that Charles was eventually diagnosed with Post Traumatic Stress Disorder (PTSD), which the psychiatrist concluded had been brought on after witnessing Marcus' death in Kuwait the year before.

At twenty years of age, and after months of counselling, it was decided that Charles would receive an honorary discharge with full pension for service to his country, as the armed forces decided he was no longer fit for duty.

Chapter 9

Charles had nowhere to go upon his exit from the army, but due to his savings he had accrued over the last few years, along with his army pension, he was able to immediately put down a deposit on a one bedroom flat. He'd opted to settle down in Lancaster after falling in love with the architecture of the city when he'd visited Marcus' grief stricken but proud parents to carry out his earlier promise.

It was here that he started to attend church again every Sunday morning after initially going in to pray for his fallen officer, and forgiveness for not being able to save the young man's life. Once again he found sanctuary in these familiar surroundings, taking comfort from the words of the Bible, always being brought back to that same verse, Isaiah 49:15.

Can a woman forget her sucking child, that she should not have compassion on the son of her womb? Yea, they may forget, yet I will not forget thee.

Charles often thought about tracking down his birth mother around this stage of his life, but just could not bring himself to do so: he could not forgive her for abandoning him, for tossing him aside as an innocent new-born, for condemning him to the torture of his youth.

Charles was at a crossroads in his life. His army career was over, yet he was still a young man and a very long way from retirement age. He pondered what he was going to do with his life from hereon in. He knew he was reasonably comfortable money wise, so he decided to explore options of future career paths, starting by visiting the local Lancaster College nearby, only a five minute walk from his new flat.

Charles decided he wasn't in a hurry to go anywhere or do anything after settling in Lancaster. With his lifelong love of animals, and his Combat Medical Technician qualifications, he decided he was going to put his two passions together and embark on a five year veterinary science degree course. Charles' mental health issues started to subside over the following few months as he found a real interest in his course, and as he was studying very long hours, he made little time for others, instead choosing to shut himself away from the world out of college hours, and opting instead to study as many books on veterinary medicine as possible. He did, however, make time a few nights a week to go to the gym; he'd recently become a member of the local leisure centre, after realising that exercise is great help in battling depression. He had missed the euphoric buzz he used to feel after his army day workouts.

Charles, being ever shy, didn't have much luck with the opposite sex, as he never knew what to say when females approached him. More often than not, he would blush and freeze if any girl showed an interest in him. True, he did go on a few dates in his first year in Lancaster, after meeting girls either in the gym or in college, but many of them never got beyond a first date, due to lots of uncomfortable silences over dinner. Charles also had a bad habit of taking them to the cinema to watch action movies so he didn't have to make conversation. Needless to say, nothing ever materialised any further, mainly due to his shyness. He wasn't particularly bothered, as he had developed serious trust issues over the past few years and could never let himself get too close to another person. He instead opted to visit 'massage' parlours and brothels to fulfil his physical needs so he didn't have to involve emotion. To him it was just a business transaction, and that suited him just fine.

This all changed during his third year of studies when, as he was walking along the long college corridor, he was left totally speechless and blown away as he noticed a young, slim, mousey haired vision of beauty walking towards him. As she approached him, his feet suddenly firmly rooted to the spot and his nostrils flared as he caught the scent of her sweet perfume. He just stood staring in awe as she flashed him a shy smile. Her skin glowed and she oozed sex appeal in a played-down, understated manner. As she passed him in the hall, he could not take his eyes off her shapely, toned legs that fell from her mid-thigh length floral dress. He practically pulled his neck muscles as he turned to take another look at her firm behind as she casually strolled further away down the corridor and out of his sight.

Charles had no clue who this girl was; he had never seen her in college before, and presumed she was a new student. But he knew he wanted to get to know her, as in that moment he felt something he had never felt before. His palms were sweaty, his stomach was in knots and his heart raced with excitement at finding out just who this girl was. He wondered if this is what being in love felt like, but couldn't be sure, as he had never experienced that feeling before. All he knew was that she was the most beautiful thing he had ever seen in his life, and told himself in that one moment that she would be the girl he would marry. He just didn't know how to make that dream become a reality yet.

Charles saw the girl on several occasions over the weeks that followed, but he could never quite muster up the courage to engage in conversation with her. However, he was pretty certain she had taken a fancy to him also, for whenever they did cross paths she would often look his way as if to gain his attention, hoping he might actually talk to her. By this point he had already found out her name — Rebecca — from one of the other students in conversation, but just couldn't find the right words whenever he came face to face with her.

All that changed one afternoon. As Charles sat studying in the library, he noticed her enter with two of her friends. But instead of studying with them, she broke away from the others and made her way over to where he was sitting.

'Do you mind if I sit here?' she asked, as she removed the seat opposite him.

'Err, no, not at all,' he nervously responded.

She flashed a clear white smile at his ever reddening face. 'Charles isn't it?'

He tried to divert his blushes by swiftly perusing through his text book that was sat open in front of him. Slowly, he looked up at her, his shifty blue eyes catching hers for an instance. He started to panic; he didn't want to get off on the wrong foot and blow any future chance of romance with the girl he had already decided was the 'one'.

He quickly composed himself, took a deep breath and replied. 'Yes, and you are Rebecca I believe?'

'Indeed I am. I see that somebody's been doing their homework?' she replied playfully.

He wasn't too sure how to respond to her question, as he did not want to come across as the sleazy stalker type.

Before any words could enter his mouth, she said, 'Relax, I'm just kidding, Charles.'

Charles immediately felt at ease as they just sat there and smiled at each other for what seemed like an age, but was really only a matter of a few short seconds. Not much studying was done by either party over the next hour, as conversation seemed to flow so freely, and Charles felt so comfortable talking with her after his initial apprehensions.

Over the course of their conversation, Charles

found himself telling Rebecca all about his time in the army, regaling in his against all odds victory not only in Kuwait, but also in the ring against the Navy boxer Tyrone Williams. He decided to omit the parts about his PTSD, the incident with Marcus Lancaster, his depression and subsequent honorary discharge... as he was aware of the stigma attached to mental health problems, and didn't want to scare her off when things were going so well.

Rebecca then told Charles all about herself and her background. He felt a slight sense of jealousy as she delighted in telling him how she grew up in a moderately affluent family home on the outskirts of Carlisle as an only daughter to a doting mother and father. Although she had longed for a sibling to play with, her parents lavished her with love and affection to try and compensate for not bearing another child. To him, she had the perfect childhood, something he had only ever dreamed of; it reminded him of the McMullens, and made him think of the life he would have had if only tragedy hadn't struck his 'mum' at a such a young age. Even though the two of them grew up less than fifty miles apart, it seemed a million miles away to Charles from the childhood he had to endure.

He never let his jealousy show, though — he was too intrigued, and held onto her every word. He could not quite believe it when she, too, explained how she had always been very shy and uncomfortable in group settings. He was also shocked to discover that she had never really had a proper boyfriend, as she had never felt a strong connection with anybody. This just added to his fascination with her, as he had somehow formed a preconception of her being a very popular girl, especially with the boys on campus. He thought he would have to vie with a long line of suitors to win her affection, but now he realised she wasn't that girl at all. This just further reaffirmed his dream of one day marrying her.

With the pair of them interacting so well, they totally forgot about the time. Charles could not quite believe just how enthusiastic Rebecca seemed to get to know him, and just how much two people from totally different backgrounds seemed to have so much in common. He did not want the conversation to end, he was quite content just looking at her and listening to every sentence she had to offer. But unfortunately, after she caught a glimpse of the overhead clock that hung on the library wall close to where they sat, she realised that she was late for her next lesson and had to make her apologies and leave. Charles, not wanting this to be the last time they conversed so meaningfully, started to get all flustered, and gingerly asked her if she would like to 'go out for a drink' with him sometime to continue where they were about to leave off.

'Are you asking me out on a date, Charles?' she asked him, a hint of a playful smile on her lips.

'Well, only if you want it to be?' he cautiously responded, not wanting her to think he had confused her friendliness with flirtations.

He waited with baited breath for her response.

'I would love to, Charles. That would be nice,' she said finally, before leaving the table and making her way towards the exit.

Charles sat there for a further ten minutes after she had left, grinning from ear to ear, lost in his detailed and analysed thoughts of the last eighty minute conversation. He could not wait till he saw her again, and he definitely believed now that he was falling in love with this perfect young lady that had just agreed to accompany him on a date.

The following week they arranged to meet up, but instead of taking Rebecca to the cinema to save from awkward silences, Charles decided to pull out all the stops; this time things were going to be different. He didn't feel an impending dread or uncertainty about the date, although he was now filled with a kind of nervous excitement. He had all kinds of ideas of what to do to make it a great first date, but he wanted to ensure it led to a second, and so forth. After careful deliberation, he decided he was going to do it the old fashioned way and take Rebecca for a picnic in the park, therefore avoiding large crowded areas like bars and clubs. It also meant that he could have her undivided attention.

He spent the days leading up to the date carefully and precisely planning what he would wear, what he would say, obsessing over every minute detail. He'd already set his heart on spending the rest of his life with her, and believed after just talking to her that one time for a short while, in Rebecca, he had found his soulmate. Charles made sure he was clean shaven, bar a little facial stubble that covered an inch long scar just along his jaw line that was a remnant of that fateful day in Kuwait; something he was self-conscious of, especially around girls. He visited his regular barber shop and had his jet black hair cut in his customary 'short back and sides' fashion, and threw on his finest jeans and shirt before adding his favourite scent. He was ready to go and meet Rebecca.

All his efforts didn't go unnoticed by Rebecca, as she too had spent the last few days leading up to it carefully pondering over what to wear etc. She was immediately put at ease when they met, though, as Charles' face said it all. His beaming smile spanned from ear to ear as he saw the slim, attractive Rebecca walk towards him, her floral print maxi dress gently billowing in the warm summer breeze, as strands of her mousey hair that she wore down casually swept across her cheeks. As he greeted her he tentatively leaned in to kiss her cheek, catching a waft of the sweet aroma of her Chanel perfume which drove his senses wild with desire.

'You look absolutely beautiful, Rebecca,' he stated.

'Thank you,' she said, blushing shyly. She was not accustomed to those kind of compliments. She then remarked on how well he looked and asked him what he had in store for the day, as he had told her it would be a surprise previously. All her anxieties quickly subsided as he produced the laden basket he had carefully hidden behind some bushes just minutes before she had arrived.

'How does a picnic in the park sound?' he asked her, praying he hadn't made a huge mistake.

'I couldn't think of anything better, Charles,' she said, secretly relieved that he hadn't planned some sort of adrenaline driven adventure day, or dinner in a posh restaurant, as she wasn't comfortable with either. But a picnic, now that was right up her street, and she loved the romantic notion behind it. She could tell Charles wasn't like all the other boys her age who had tried it on, to no avail, by trying to take her out to the pubs and bars in the deluded hope of getting her drunk. They had wanted her to let down her guard and become somebody's one night stand. She knew that with Charles, things would be different, and she looked forward to the day ahead.

The date was a success from beginning to end, and the pair talked and laughed at length about everything and anything over the food he had prepared — they even had a bottle of champagne to accompany their feast. They sat there in the park for the majority of the day and totally put the world to rights, as if they had known each other for years. They both felt a strong connection to one another and sensed that this could be the beginning of something special.

As Charles leaned in to give Rebecca a goodnight kiss after walking her back to her halls of residence that evening, she melted in his embrace, totally smitten and absorbed in his apparent charm and gentlemanly ways. They kissed on the doorstep for a solid five minutes like a couple of love-struck teenagers tangled in a modern day Romeo and Juliet fantasy, hoping they wouldn't be caught by the on-site security guard. Both of them did not want the evening to come to an end, before finally letting go of one another and bidding each other goodnight.

Over the weeks and months that followed, their feelings for one another and relationship grew deeper and stronger and Rebecca didn't hesitate when Charles suggested she move in with him into his flat. He even let her add a touch of femininity to his meticulously regimented, minimalist decorated man cave, with flowers, ornaments, pictures and fluffy cushions now adorning once bare walls and furniture. Life was actually good for Charles at that point, and he was feeling positive about his future with Rebecca by his side.

It was now 1995 and Charles and Rebecca had a remaining two years of studies left at Lancaster. It was at this point that the couple started making plans for the future, with Rebecca keen to return back to Cumbria to be close to her parents upon finishing her studies. Charles, on the other hand, wasn't as keen, for Cumbria obviously held unwanted memories of his past — a past he wanted to remain forgotten.

Charles and Rebecca had their ups and downs over the two years that followed like any couple do. Usually the arguments were down to Charles not wanting to commit to returning to Cumbria, and the fact that Charles would never discuss his past. Instead, he chose to lie to Rebecca about his childhood, telling her his parents died in a car accident and he was raised as an only child by his grandmother who had also passed away, and he would always disengage whenever Rebecca brought the topic up. It was just before they both graduated in 1997 that the couple came close to separating as Rebecca was adamant she would be returning north with or without Charles. Charles deliberated long and hard about his options, and he quickly realised that he did not want to be without Rebecca, the girl who had given him a new meaning to his life and helped him put the troubles of his past behind him. Whichever way he looked at it, he just could not imagine a future without her in it.

It was on August 11th of that year, on Charles' twenty-fifth birthday to be exact, and a month before graduation, that Charles, after coming to the conclusion that he could not live without Rebecca, decided that now was the right time to propose to her. He decided to recreate their first date and took Rebecca back to the exact same spot where they had sat just over two years before, and produced the same picnic basket and contents as the last time. The only difference was that this time, there was an extra parcel that Rebecca instantly spied as they unloaded the basket onto the blanket.

'What is this, Charles?' she asked excitedly.

'Open it up and find out,' was all he could reply, as the butterflies in his stomach started to become more prevalent.

As she opened the claret coloured velveteen box, and laid her eyes on the diamond-laden golden band before her, tears instantly fell down her cheeks.

'Is this what I think it is?' she asked, already knowing the answer, but just wanting to be a hundred per cent certain.

Charles then took her now trembling hand in his, and with a shaky voice, uttered the words, 'Rebecca, I've known from the moment I met you that you are the one I want to grow old with and spend the rest of my life with. Will you make me the happiest man alive and be my wife? I promise to always love you and be there for you no matter where we live, and I will always be by your side.'

Rebecca, ecstatic by this point, threw her arms around him. 'Of course I will Charles, I don't ever want to be without you!'

The couple spent the rest of the day in blissful harmony talking about the future, and Charles informed her that he had spoken to an estate agent and that his flat was going up for sale as soon as it had been evaluated, so hopefully they would be able to afford a deposit for a new home and make plans to leave Lancaster. The couple set about looking for properties in the Carlisle area the very next day.

Unfortunately, it wasn't all plain sailing. Every property they viewed over the following weeks were slightly out of their price range; they had discussed starting a family once they had married and wanted a three bedroom house that they could immediately turn into a family home. So when they saw the slightly rundown cottage in the Newcastleton countryside, they both instantly fell in love with the peaceful surroundings. They couldn't refuse to bid for the property; its asking price was low due to the dilapidated state of it, but this didn't put the two off. They finally managed to land the property and Charles immediately set about renovating it over the following months whilst searching for work in the many surrounding veterinary surgeries.

The house was coming along nicely, with Charles doing the majority of the cosmetic work himself to save on costs, whilst Rebecca worked long hours to support the pair of them and help save toward their impending wedding. Charles then found work at a small veterinary practice in Longtown, just eight miles north of Carlisle. The young couple's future was looking bright; they were settling in to working life and country living with relative ease, and gradually became a part of the local community.

Charles and Rebecca exchanged vows in front of a small gathering of friends and family — mainly the bride's, with the odd exception of a couple of Charles' old army buddies — in February 1999, Valentine's day to be exact, just fifteen months after moving into their new home. Life was all but complete for the newlyweds; all that was left now was to start a family of their own. Charles dreamt of one day having a son of his own, to shower him with love and affection and give him a stability that he never had, whereas

83

Rebecca secretly hoped for a little girl. The couple had already decided that they would have two children when the time was right, so they hoped they would have one of each.

Charles, by this point, had all but forgotten his childhood and any ambitions of one day contacting his biological mother. Instead, he focused on being the best husband and provider he could be, preferring to look towards the future rather than dwell upon his miserable past. However, not through lack of trying, it took over a whole year for Rebecca to finally conceive. The couple were both relieved and overjoyed when Molly finally entered into the world in the spring of 2001. Although Charles had secretly hoped for a boy, he was overcome and overwhelmed with emotion when he held his daughter for the very first time; his tears of joy were mingled with tears of sadness as he wondered desperately how his mother could have given him away when all he wanted to do was keep his daughter in his arms and never let go. He vowed to his new-born and wife, then and there, that he would never let them down.

Charles and Rebecca thrived as parents, and loved every minute of raising their daughter. Rebecca only went back to work part-time after her maternity leave — a luxury they could afford now with Charles working full-time on good wages and with a relatively small mortgage. Molly couldn't have wanted for anything more from her doting parents.

By the time Molly turned four, Rebecca was once again feeling broody and decided now was the right time to have the second child they had talked about previously. This time they conceived relatively quickly and Fiona came into the world the following year in 2006. Again, although it wasn't the son he had wished for, Charles and Rebecca felt that their lives were now complete. Rebecca never went back to work after her maternity leave this time, as the couple decided that, due to them being reasonably comfortable financially and with Molly just starting school, that it would be better all-round if Rebecca was close by in case of emergency. That way, she could relish every moment of Fiona's infant years — a luxury she missed out on with Molly due to work commitments.

By the time Fiona had turned three, Charles decided that there was just one thing missing from the family home: the one thing that had brought him joy in his childhood. He surprised the girls one evening when he brought home a black and white Border collie puppy. The two young girls instantly fell in love with her — even more so when their father informed them that they could choose her name. After much deliberation and bickering between the two girls, with Fiona wanting to name her anything from 'Princess' to 'Stinky', it was finally decided to go with Molly's suggestion of 'Tess', and the family home was now complete.

Charles and Rebecca encouraged the two girls to go after whatever dreams they had as they were growing up, and actively supported them through whatever ambitions they held. The parents never hesitated when Molly stated that she would like her own horse after really enjoying previous riding lessons she had received, and falling in love with all things equestrian from a young age. Due to Fiona's extroverted nature and natural performing ability, she was signed up to every performing arts class in the area from a young age, and the couple did everything in their capabilities to make it a happy, loving childhood for their daughters. Their efforts were rewarded after Molly's success in the junior equestrian competition.

Chapter 10

A month had now passed since Lucy Mitchell's disappearance had dominated the local news, and it was back to business as normal for Charles at the practice. A new year, a new start he thought to himself as 2014 got underway.

He tried to push any thoughts of the dead schoolgirl to the back of his mind and concentrate on his heavy workload from now on, and managed to do just that for the next couple of weeks, but the thoughts of his actions quickly resurfaced. His resentment towards his mother and Mr Beattie soon weighed heavy upon his mind once more. Once again, revenge was fixed firmly on his agenda.

It was on a cold, dark February evening, whilst Charles was supposedly working late, that his overwhelming urges took a hold of him yet again. Unbeknown to Rebecca, Charles had been leaving the practice early all week, telling his secretary Linda that he was out on house calls, but he was really scouring areas afield in the veterinary practice's van for potential victims.

It didn't take him long, as that evening whilst driving around the Penrith area some nineteen miles south of Carlisle, he spotted a young, blonde haired girl who looked no more than fourteen or fifteen years old. She looked to be in some form of distress as she sat sobbing near a bus stop just on the outskirts of town with make up running down the side of her cheeks. Charles didn't want to miss this opportunity and decided to pull over down a dimly lit side street and make his way out of the vehicle and approach the girl.

He spoke to her in a soft voice so as not to be intimidating. 'Are you ok?'

The girl looked up with tear-filled eyes. 'I've lost my p-purse,' she said, in between sobs, 'and the d-driver wouldn't let me on the bus. My parents will be s-so worried if I don't make it home on time.'

Charles couldn't believe his luck. 'Which way are you heading?'

He had already decided that no matter which way she told him, he was going to be going the same way as her so would therefore offer her a ride home.

When the girl informed him that she lived only three miles outside of Penrith, Charles volunteered to take her home.

The girl, still fighting back tears, thought for a few moments. She knew full well that accepting lifts from strangers was totally against everything she had ever been told. Then again, she also didn't want to offend what could genuinely be a good Samaritan offering her a solution to her problems. She decided to respectfully decline his offer.

Charles, sensing her anxieties and not wanting to raise suspicion, informed the girl that he himself was a father to two young daughters and would hate the thought of them being stranded without anyone to lend a hand. With that, she reassessed the situation with her parents worry factored in and reluctantly decided to accept his offer, and made her way over to where Charles had parked the van.

Charles, always the gentleman, even approached the passenger side first and opened the door for her in a welcoming manner, offering her further reassurance that it was safe and ok. As he closed the door after her, Charles made his way towards the rear of the van, opting to take the long way round to the driver's side. As he approached the back of the vehicle and out of the girl's sight, he quickly reached down into his jacket pocket and took out a handkerchief and bottle of chloroform, and swiftly removed the cap. He proceeded to empty a substantial amount into the handkerchief before placing the bottle back into his pocket and making his way to the driver's side door.

Charles offered her a reassuring smile upon entering the vehicle, and insisted 'safety first' as he asked her to put on her seatbelt. The girl, totally at ease now due to his apparent charming nature, turned to locate her seatbelt as he had asked, and in that split second her back was turned to him, Charles pounced in a cold, calculated manner, as he grabbed her forcefully around her shoulder and chest with his left arm whilst placing the handkerchief over her nose and mouth with his right hand.

The girl didn't stand a chance against the much stronger man, and she was all but unconscious before she even had time to panic. Charles held his position for a few seconds longer than necessary just to be sure she wouldn't wake anytime soon. Once her body went limp in his arms, he casually leant over her and placed the seatbelt around her so to avoid being pulled over by the police. He then proceeded to start the engine and drive away in a calm fashion without anybody even realising what had just happened.

A huge smug grin enveloped Charles' face as he exited the roundabout leaving Penrith and entered the M6 northbound into a sea of traffic, as he knew the further away he got, the less likely it would be that he would be pulled over by the police. The further north he drove, his adrenaline levels started to subside, and his thoughts were now becoming more consumed by lust as he recollected the last look in Lucy's dying eyes, and how she would have been thankful that he chose her. He became more and more aroused as he also remembered how empowered he had felt as he extinguished the helpless little whore's life at his hands and the control it gave him. He relished the prospect of doing it again.

As Charles exited the motorway and joined the much quieter A7 northbound, he knew he was nearly home and dry, as it was only a few more miles before he would exit the road at Canonbie, and take the even less frequently used B roads that led a long, winding path straight to the heart of Kielder.

All thoughts of his wife and daughters were long gone in Charles' mind, as the anticipation of what was to come brought unrivalled excitement to him. He couldn't refrain himself from running his free left hand through the unconscious girl's soft blonde hair, down over her bosom, and finally into her lap, resting it on her thigh, just below her black, pleated skirt, biting and licking his lips whilst doing so. Not long to go now, he thought to himself as he neared the layby he had previously used. Now there was only the small matter of transporting her lifeless body through the pitch black, dense forestry. Normally he wouldn't be in there so late, but he knew he had no alternative than to operate under the cover of darkness to avoid suspicion and detection from anyone else.

As Charles exited the vehicle, he was startled by the headlights of another vehicle approaching where he was standing, and even more surprised when he spotted the indicator signalling to turn into the same layby. His adrenaline kicked in sharply as the vehicle drew ever closer, and he reached into his pocket and removed the bottle of chloroform and handkerchief, thinking that he might possibly have to act fast if somebody was to question his motive for being in such a remote spot in the pitch black darkness.

As the other vehicle pulled up alongside Charles, his apprehensions were quickly squashed; it was just a tourist asking for directions, lost in a maze of rarely used B roads and wanting his help. Charles dropped the chloroform and handkerchief back into his pocket and made his way towards the driver's open window, totally blocking him from potentially seeing the young girl slouched, unconscious, in the passenger seat, and calmly instructed the lost man on how to get back onto the main road. Charles breathed a sigh of relief as the man thanked him and casually pulled away without ever questioning his reasons for being there. Back to the matter at hand, he thought to himself as he removed the comatose girl from the van and cable-tied her hands and feet. He flung her over his shoulder and made his way through the short field that led into the cover of the tree line and along his own secret pathway he had already established, away from any prying eyes.

Not much further now! He was nearing the hidden chamber in which Lucy's body remained undiscovered. But he wasn't prepared for what happened next, as the girl over his shoulder started to wake, and in a groggy stupor and blind panic, she let out a deafening high pitched scream that brought ringing to his ears. Shit! Rookie error — why hadn't he bothered to gag her when he tied her limbs together?! He quickly threw the girl to the floor then tore off her cardigan and tied it around her mouth tightly to silence her. He then dragged her the remaining 200 yards by her hair as she struggled fruitlessly to get to her feet, away from his grasp. She desperately tried to wriggle out of the ties for a few moments as Charles removed the foliage and debris that covered the underground dungeon that contained Lucy. The more she tried to escape, the deeper the restraints dug into her skin.

As Charles threw open the entrance to the pit, nothing could have prepared him for the overwhelming, putrid stench that hit his nostrils from Lucy's heavily decomposing corpse. He turned and vomited. The stench hit the girl's nostrils; she knew that something awful was down there, but due to her position she could not see what. She just knew when she caught the stranger's eyes that whatever it was, it did not bode well for her, and all she could do was pray that he had a change of heart and took pity on her as she desperately tried to break free.

Charles knew though that he could not leave this one till the next day down in that hole with the rotting corpse beside her — he would have to act fast and complete the 'job' he had set out to do. Besides, she was just another filthy little whore anyway, and should be grateful that he was going to end her miserable, pathetic, worthless existence!

As he approached her his excitement levels increased. He hadn't bothered bringing the ketamine this time, as he wanted this next victim to be aware of everything that was going to be happening in those final moments, unlike Lucy, who only woke in her last few dying seconds.

He slowly calmed a little. Stroking her hair, he ran the back of his hand over her cheeks, softly wiping away the tears that ran down her face. Charles was now in a warped sense of reality, and she knew this, as he came down to her level and planted a soft kiss on her cheek.

'Don't worry, Mother. This will all be over very soon and you'll be at peace, just you wait and see,' he whispered in her ear.

Then as quick as a flash, his whole demeanour changed as he forcefully tore away her remaining clothes and pulled out his pocket knife to cut away her leg restraints — he wanted to get in between her legs, so as to look into her eyes like before.

As Charles proceeded to force himself on the helpless, petrified child, he started to repeat the words over and over again in his head: yea, they may forget, yet I will not forget thee. Every time he looked down upon her, her face became distorted, and images of Lucy flashed before him, then faceless images of the mother he imagined. He was now totally lost in his own delusions and hadn't even realised that he had already ended the girl's life whilst strangling her until after he had climaxed. Once again he felt cheated that he hadn't been 'in the moment' when she had passed due to his preoccupations and visions. However, he still once again placed a soft kiss on her forehead.

'Goodnight, Mother.'

He was late — Rebecca might start asking questions. Charles quickly grabbed the lifeless girl's legs and dragged her over to the open pit, casually rolling her body until she landed on Lucy's rotting remains.

He looked at the two of them for a few seconds, feeling proud of his work, before re-closing the entrance, once again disguising it with forestry. This time, he ensured the camouflage was denser and thicker than before, as he wasn't intending to come back there from now on. He double checked that he hadn't left any clues or items of clothing lying around, and once he was happy in his own mind that he had covered his tracks, he proceeded to leave the burial site, making his way back to the van. Once again, he concocted a story to relay to the waiting Rebecca upon returning home; fortunately there was no blood this time, as he hadn't beat the girl as he had previously, so it was just a case of straightening up his clothing and hair before entering the house.

'Hey, I was wondering what time you would be home, mister?' Rebecca said to her now weary-looking husband. 'I've been trying to call you for ages and got nothing but voicemail.'

'Sorry Hun,' he replied. 'I got held up with call outs and forgot to charge my phone this morning so the battery has died.'

'That's ok, I just wanted to know what time you would be home for dinner. Yours is in the microwave as we started without you when I couldn't reach you.'

'Thanks, I'll have it once I've showered and changed.'

He made his way down the hall and towards the bedroom to get out of his clothes. Eager to remove any scent that might linger on him from the girl, he stepped into the en-suite shower, feeling the hot water slamming into his aching body.

'Does that feel better?' Rebecca asked him, as he made his way back towards the kitchen in his dressing gown and slippers.

'Yes thanks,' came his reply; as he was too tired to engage in any kind of meaningful conversation.

Rebecca, sensing his lethargy, instructed her husband to take a seat while she brought him his dinner. Charles didn't need any further encouragement and made his way towards the sofa in the warm, cosy sitting room. He instantly put on the news channel on the television, checking to see if there was already any news on the missing girl from Penrith. There was nothing as of yet, and Charles seemed to become agitated, as he secretly wanted to revel in his twisted delusional brilliance. He knew it would just be a matter of time though before the media try and locate the girl once they realised she wouldn't be turning up at home.

He quickly changed the channel as Rebecca brought his dinner through to where he was sitting, accompanied by his customary glass of red wine. It wasn't long after he had finished his meal and wine that Charles fell asleep on the sofa, exhausted after his rollercoaster ride of a day. As he lay there on the sofa softly snoring, his oblivious wife lovingly placed a blanket over him and continued to take care of domestic duties. She did not want to disturb him; she knew he must be worn out due to the long hours he had been recently putting into the practice.

***

The next morning started off as usual, with Rebecca up first preparing breakfast and packed lunches for the girls, and morning coffee for her sleeping husband. As he awoke, Charles once again made his way towards the TV and placed the news channel on yet again, but still nothing of the missing girl. Charles appeared baffled and started to question whether it had actually happened or if it had all been just a dream.

Rebecca, sensing something wasn't quite right, asked Charles if there was something wrong.

'Oh no, sorry dear, I was just checking to see if the weather forecast was on, as I heard somewhere that there could be possible floods approaching,' he replied casually.

She never questioned his response, as it seemed a genuine concern with the house being right next to the river Teviot. Charles then finished his coffee and breakfast before taking Tess for her morning walk. Upon returning he began to get ready, then gave Rebecca a kiss before setting off for work.

As he entered the van he instinctively put CFM on the radio, hoping there would be some news, but once again there was nothing as he made his morning drive into work. The day seemed to drag on as he became more and more agitated at the practice. Even Linda sensed something wasn't quite right, as he had been snapping at her all day over the slightest of things. It angered him that nothing had been reported and nobody yet knew of her disappearance.

The longer the day went on, the more frustrated he became. What if he was to take another? Maybe then he would receive the exposure his work deserved. After all, he was fulfilling a public service in ridding the world of worthless little whores! Charles made his mind up there and then that his next victim would come sooner rather than later — but this time she would be disposed of somewhere she would be discovered!

As he left the practice reasonably early again that day, he was unsure of which direction he was heading, but for some reason he was drawn in the direction of Wigton, specifically near to where Mr Beattie lived at Haywood farm. He seethed as he passed along the main road, thinking back to the catalyst that unlocked all these deeply buried emotions that had recently resurfaced. He promised himself he would be back for the farmer as he slowly passed the farm and proceeded to head back in the direction of Carlisle.

Under the cover of a dark winter night, he purposefully stalked the small surrounding villages that scattered around his route back, intent on finding another 'chosen one' to be honoured by a fateful meeting with him. As luck would have it, that opportunity presented itself as he saw a girl break away from a small group of her peers and make her way on foot towards a quiet country lane, possibly making her way home to the tiny village of Great Orton just six miles outside of Carlisle. He couldn't be quite sure of her age, as unlike the others, she was not wearing a school uniform and was possibly slightly older due to the makeup that was plastered all over her face. He thought that maybe she was returning from college; she was likely no older than eighteen. Not his usual age range, but she'd do. He knew another opportunity like this might not present itself.

As he approached her he was initially going to offer her a lift, but he did not want to scare her off so chose instead to pull up alongside her and engage her in conversation by asking for directions to a non-existent farm nearby. All it took was her to lean slightly towards the open window to speak to him... he pounced. He grabbed her by her long ponytail with his outstretched right hand and shoved the chloroform-soaked handkerchief over her nose and mouth with his left without even having to exit the vehicle. He knew he had to act quickly so as not to be detected; as soon as he felt her legs buckle due to the inhalation of the anaesthetic, he got out of the van, slid open the side door and lifted her into the cage usually reserved for animals. He scanned the area to see if anybody had witnessed what had just happened and saw nothing but high hedges and greenery as he got back into the van and calmly drove away.

Panic started to set in at this point, as it suddenly dawned on him that due to his frustrations, he had not meticulously planned this far ahead unlike the previous two victims, and he was unsure where to head to next. All he knew was that he had to end her life and leave her in a place where her body would be discovered relatively promptly. His mind raced as he aimlessly drove around the boroughs of Carlisle, desperately thinking of somewhere he could finish his task and dispose of the body without being seen by prying eyes — or the many of the CCTV cameras that operate in the area.

He tried to narrow possible dumping sites down to areas on the outskirts of the city, possibly near running water to help wash away any forensic evidence he may accidentally leave behind. He decided to pull over for a few moments to gather his thoughts and recalled seeing another quiet little layby just outside of Wetheral, a small village again located in the surrounding areas of Carlisle. He knew that the river Eden ran through it, as he and Rebecca had walked along its banks on a couple of occasions after eating in the local pub every now and again.

The coast appeared to be clear as he stopped and parked the van under the large trees that ran alongside the river banks. He sat for a few minutes just to make sure, and contemplated his next move. He'd already decided that he couldn't afford for her to wake up like the girl the night before so, as he did with Lucy, he injected another five-millilitre barrel of Ketamine into her whilst she lay in the van's cage. He decided the time was right to move her down to the river bank and out of sight of any potential passers-by. He knew he would have to get this over with quickly, and made light work of removing her clothing before violating her unconscious young body.

There was to be no profanities or talking of any kind on this occasion though, as he could not risk the possibility of somebody overhearing him — this time he did not have the luxury of nothingness for miles around. The only words that were uttered this night were the customary 'Good night, Mother, sweet dreams' that he whispered to her as he planted yet another soft kiss on the now dead girl's forehead before rolling her down the embankment and hearing her body splash into the fast flowing river. Let's see if this one goes unreported, he thought.

***

His two daughters were still up as he arrived home earlier than the previous night, and Fifi instantly greeted her daddy with a big hug as she jumped up into his arms. Rebecca offered him a huge smile upon witnessing this, seeming happy that she might actually get to spend a few extra precious hours with her husband for a change.

After a few short moments of the girls greeting their recently absent father, with even Molly showing an interest, their mother instructed the girls to go get their pyjamas on and prepare themselves for bed.

'What's the hurry?' Charles asked Rebecca as the kids made their way towards their bedrooms to change.

'Let's just say that I have got a surprise in store for you after dinner and once the kids are asleep,' Rebecca replied.

Charles smiled. 'I suppose I better go for a shower and get cleaned up before dinner then shall I?'

She nodded her head and offered a cheeky wink as he started to make his way towards their bedroom. Upon exiting the shower and putting on some fresh clothes, Charles made his way into his daughters' separate bedrooms. Firstly he gave Molly a goodnight kiss, as she insisted she was too old for bedtime stories, then he tucked Fiona in for the night with her favourite soft toy and book. As he made his approach back to where his wife was making dinner, Rebecca began to make casual conversation with him.

'Did you happen to catch the local news this evening by any chance?'

Charles, sensing something wasn't quite right and feeling a little bit as though he was being quizzed by her, sat upright. 'No why? Should I have?'

'Oh no, I just thought you might have seen that another young girl has gone missing. This time from the Penrith area.'

'No, I haven't heard anything, love,' he responded.

'Well, they're saying it's too early to tell at this moment in time, but the police have said that there is a very slim chance that this may be related to that poor girl Lucy who disappeared before Christmas from Gretna. What is the world coming to when teenage girls are randomly being snatched off the streets? I won't be letting our two out of my sight from now on. I can only imagine what those poor families must be going through right now!'

'Yeah, god only knows how they must be feeling.'

After the couple had finished eating their dinner they nestled down together on the sofa for the evening. After about an hour or so had passed, Charles noticed a familiar figure appear on the television screen who he recognised instantly as Jennifer Metcalfe, the slim, young journalist who had reported on the disappearance of Lucy Mitchell. His eyes lit up as he awaited what she had to say on the second missing schoolgirl.

'I am here now in Penrith, where police are investigating the disappearance of fourteen-year-old schoolgirl Sarah Davidson, who hasn't been seen since yesterday evening. Her parents are deeply worried and are appealing for her to return home. If anybody knows where she is, could they please come forward and cooperate with the police and help them in their investigations? This is Jennifer Metcalfe, reporting live from Penrith.'

Even though it was brief, Charles could barely

contain the smug grin that enveloped his face: he would finally get the recognition his work deserved. Maybe now they might start to take him seriously! The thrill of it all started to make him feel aroused, and about five minutes later he turned to his wife with a hungry look in his eyes.

'So, what was it you had in store for me tonight anyway?' he asked her in a playful manner.

'Follow me and find out,' she told him.

She got up and took his hand, then led him down the corridor towards their bedroom and marital bed.

***

The next morning Charles chose to take a different route to work, opting to go the long way around and pass through the picturesque little village of Wetheral he had left under the cover of darkness the previous evening. Much to his dismay, there was no activity near the site of where he had dumped the girl's body, but he knew he didn't have time to sit around and wait and potentially be reported for acting suspiciously, so he left the area and headed the few short miles to work. It was just after lunch that Charles was informed of the third girl's body being discovered.

'Have you heard the news about that missing girl?' Linda asked with a sad look on her face.

Charles, just realising that he hadn't had the radio on today as he had been far too busy catching up on jobs, replied to his secretary by saying, 'Yes, it's terrible, that poor young girl from Penrith. I saw it at home last night. It's an awful shame. Has she turned up yet?'

'No, not her Charles, this is a different girl. They're saying that a body has been found by the side of the river Eden by a passing jogger, and although they are not quite sure who she is yet, they have said that she definitely does not match the description of Sarah, the girl from Penrith.'

'Oh, bloody hell! That doesn't sound good.' He quickly returned to his office, immediately putting his radio on to see if he could hear any more news on the recent discovery. A few more hours passed before the police finally confirmed that the body was that of seventeen-year-old Carlisle college student, Amber Thompson, who had not returned home the night before. The report continued to say that the police were now contemplating the possibility that Amber's body and the disappearance of Sarah Davidson and Lucy Mitchell may be connected.

There was a media frenzy over the following days, with dozens of journalists and television crews desperately trying to get an insight into the Cumbria police's official line on the matter, and any information they may have on leads in their investigations. On top of that, there was a community on edge and starting to become extremely hostile, with demonstrations taking place not just outside Carlisle police headquarters, with families of the victims leading the protests, wanting answers as to how this was allowed to happen in their usually peaceful, and generally safe communities.

As the mob grew and became more and more impatient with the lack of information, Cumbria's Chief Inspector, Ian Messenger, decided that the time was now right to call a press conference and let the families and media know exactly how they were going to be handling the case, and inform them of any leads, which, as of this point they did not have.

***

It was on February 16th 2014, just two days after Charles and Rebecca had celebrated their fifteen year anniversary, that the press conference took place in Carlisle police headquarters conference room. The families of all the three girls were invited, along with a selection of local and national newspaper journalists and a couple of television crews. Chief Inspector Messenger began the proceedings by welcoming everybody there under such difficult circumstances, and assured the families that the case had become their number one priority since the discovery of Amber's body. It was at this point that he introduced the man sat to his right, Detective Inspector Steven Taylor — the lead detective assigned to the case.

It was at this point that Detective Taylor stood and addressed the tense crowd before him. He started by thanking everybody in attendance and went on to reassure them that he and his team of detectives would be working around the clock to catch the person or persons who murdered Amber Thompson; although they were unsure of there being any connection between her death and the disappearance of Lucy Mitchell and Sarah Davidson, they would be exploring all possibilities and avenues of investigations.

'We *will* find the perpetrators of these crimes, and they *will* be punished,' he said passionately. 'I'll now take questions from the audience.'

The first question to be directed at him was from a very emotional Mr Thompson, Amber's distraught father.

'Do you have any idea who abducted and murdered our daughter?' he choked, as he clutched the hand of his wife, who sat beside him.

'I'm so sorry to say Mr Thompson, but at this moment in time, I'm afraid we cannot shed any light on who committed this terrible act. What I can say, however, is that right now my team has enlisted the help of a psychological profiler to try and help us narrow down the search, and hopefully offer us some fresh ideas. The forensics team are painstakingly inspecting every inch of the site where Amber's body was discovered, and they will hopefully offer more evidence to help with our investigation.'

The next question came from the mother of Lucy

Mitchell. 'Why is it that, nearly two months after our daughter was taken, we are still no further forward in discovering what exactly happened to her. Do you honestly believe that the disappearance of all three girls are connected?'

'Well, I can't comment on any investigations into Lucy's disappearance, Mrs Mitchell. Until Amber's tragic discovery, along with Sarah Davidson going missing the night before, Lucy's case was being handled by Dumfries and Galloway constabulary. It's only since then that my team and I have had any correspondence with them, as it was believed that Lucy's disappearance was an isolated incident, with no evidence to suggest otherwise. However, I can assure you that both constabularies will be working alongside each other from hereon in, and sharing any fresh information any of us might bring to light.'

The following question came from the journalist who had been covering the story from the onset.

'Jennifer Metcalfe, Border TV. Without wishing to sound insensitive, Detective, could you give us your honest opinion as to whether or not you believe the missing girls Lucy Mitchell and Sarah Davidson have fallen victim to the same fate as Amber, and have yet to be discovered? Or do you still hold any hope of them turning up unharmed?'

'That's a very good question, Miss Metcalfe,' Taylor responded, 'and the honest answer is that at this moment in time it is too early to tell.'

This started a whole barrage of questions from the media. The term 'serial killer' started to be thrown around the room, prompting Chief Inspector Messenger to interject.

'There is no evidence whatsoever to suggest that this was the work of a serial killer,' he said firmly. 'As of yet, we have only discovered one body and there's no solid evidence to link the three girls. Any speculation to the contrary of this will only cause widespread panic and hysteria to the local communities, and may have a negative effect on the investigation.'

It was at this point that he decided to call a halt to the conference and informed everybody that as soon as they discovered any more details they would be released to the families and the press in due time. The two detectives then swiftly removed themselves from the room, leaving the remaining police officers to restore order and disperse the crowd calmly.

As the two of them returned to their respective offices, Chief Inspector Messenger turned to his colleague.

'We need answers, and we need them fast, Detective Taylor. If there is any chance whatsoever that we have a serial killer on our hands then we need to bring this reign of terror to an end before we lose the trust of the community and have a civil outcry on our streets!'

'I assure you, sir, I'm going to do everything in my power to solve this case. You have my word on that.'

'Let's just hope that is enough, Detective,' Messenger said gravely, before returning to his own office and firmly closing the door behind him.

Taylor's thoughts were a blur. Shit. Where should he even begin? He made his way towards his department and team to see if there was any new leads.

Chief Inspector Messenger had placed a lot of trust in Taylor by placing him in charge of his CID department only a few years earlier. He'd chosen him from an outside department as opposed to promoting from within, and rightly so, as Taylor came from Hyndburn in Lancashire's Serious Crime Task Force with a glowing reference after gaining a great reputation and making a name for himself in the 90s. He and his partner had solved the gangland murder of Jonny 'The Butcher' Balmer, the head of a serious organised crime gang in Lancashire. He went on to run the division for a number of years before opting for a more 'peaceful' life, heading north to Carlisle's

CID department in Cumbria. He'd never thought for one moment that he would be faced with the biggest case of his career, tracking a possible serial killer, but he was confident that he was the right man for the job and threw himself into his work.

It was a hive of activity in the department, with people desperately trying to filter through the hundreds of calls being received by the hour offering clues as to who might be behind all this. Most of them were from genuinely concerned citizens offering any scrap of information they might think relevant, but there were also a number of fake callers and cranks proclaiming to be the killer due to the publicity the case was getting nationwide.

Taylor knew that he had the whole country, let alone the county, watching intently to see where this would lead. It was at this point that, whilst Detective Taylor was conversing with the forensic team who had been working the site where Amber's body was discovered, one of his colleagues introduced him to the psychological profiler who had been called in to help build up an understanding of who they might actually be up against.

'Sir, this is Miss Georgina Riley, she is going to be working alongside you in helping to build a picture of the person or persons we are looking for.'

'Please, just call me George or Georgie, Detective,' she said to Taylor.

Taylor, taken aback by the stunning redhead he was faced with, tried desperately to remain composed. Although he was a married man, he immediately felt a strong attraction towards the woman before him, and stuttered slightly as he formally introduced himself and dismissed his colleague.

He waited for his colleague to leave, watching Miss Riley intently.

'You've turned up at just the right time, Miss Riley', he informed her. 'I was just about to get some answers from forensics regarding any evidence from the discovery site.'

'Please, lead the way then. I'm here to help and assist you in any which way I can.'

'So, you were saying?' Taylor spoke to the forensic expert in a matter of fact manner, immediately trying to impress Miss Riley.

'Yes, as I was saying. Pathology have confirmed that Amber was murdered sometime on the early evening of her disappearance, possibly between 7 and 10pm. But due to the fact that she wasn't discovered until the next day, and adding to that fact that there was heavy rain fall that evening, we estimate that her body could have travelled anywhere between two to six miles on that particular stretch of river.

However, we did discover a couple of miles upstream what appears to be a partial footprint on the river embankment. It is in the process of being analysed, and looks to be about a size ten or eleven, although that hasn't been confirmed yet.'

'Was that all?' Taylor asked.

'Well, from the bruises on her neck, and burst capillaries around her eyes and cheeks, we have been able to confirm the cause of death as asphyxiation caused by strangulation. Another thing that will interest you is that toxicology also confirmed that she had a large quantity of ketamine in her system — far more than would be used recreationally — and also a trace of chloroform was detected.'

'What about fibres or DNA traces?' Taylor then asked, becoming more and more intrigued by these discoveries.

'Again, unfortunately due to her being in the water for possibly up to fifteen hours, we were unable to find any traces of fibres, or semen for that matter. Which is disappointing, because due to the bruises around her groin, it would appear that forced intercourse took place. Also I might add, she must've been unconscious at the time the rape took place as there was no sign of any struggle, and no skin or fibres under her fingernails.'

'Thanks.'

Taylor and Georgie then left and made their way towards the vending machine to get a cup of coffee, then into his office.

As they entered his office, Taylor pulled up a seat for her and asked Georgie for her opinion on what had just been discovered.

'Well, I will start by saying that it doesn't bode well for the other two missing girls if these cases are related.'

'And what may I ask leads you to that conclusion?' he questioned.

'Going off what I have just heard, it would appear that we are dealing with an extremely well-organised and calculated individual, with a good knowledge of the local area. And if it is the same person that has taken all three girls, I would say that the other two bodies just remain to be discovered.'

'Shit!' Taylor brooded for a moment before sighing. 'Please continue.'

'Again, and it's only a theory at this point, but, if they are related, then the common denominator is the fact that they are all teenage girls.'

'I could have told you that!' he snapped at her in frustration.

'Do you want my help or not, Detective?' she retorted fiercely.

Taylor then mumbled an apology under his breath and politely asked her once more to finish what she was saying.

'As I was saying; the fact that all three are all teenage girls, alongside the fact that Amber appears to have been raped, it would suggest that it was a male. I would hazard a guess at saying a white male between the age of thirty-five and fifty given his extensive knowledge of the different areas. I would also go out on a limb and say that he probably lives and works somewhere within a region of fifty miles from here.

'I would say that he is possibly a little socially inept,

and maybe a bit of an introvert who struggles to speak to members of the opposite sex — he may possibly even have some sort of an affliction that causes him to be self-conscious. As for work, I would also maybe say it is someone who travels a fair bit, possibly a truck driver or cabbie maybe. There's just one thing I can't quite get my head round though...'

'Which is?' Taylor excitedly fired back at her.

'The ketamine and chloroform. How did he gain access to these? I feel as though I'm missing something.'

'What about his background?'

'Well, he is careful by nature and possibly has knowledge of forensics; he drugged her before the rape, and also submerged her in water to try and rid her of any evidence. I would say that there is a real possibility that he has maybe been trialled or even prosecuted for previous sexual or violence related offences, or possibly been treated for anger issues.'

'So what you are telling me is that this doesn't look like it's going to be a one off, and you honestly think he will strike again, if he hasn't already?' Taylor asks her, fearfully awaiting her response.

'What I am telling you, Detective, is that I believe he will not only strike again, but that he is developing a real taste for it and is enjoying his work. I don't believe for one second that it was by coincidence that Amber's body was discovered: I think that he has grown confident since the first two girls, and that he wanted Amber to be found. He is secretly loving the attention the media have placed on the case, as he does not know how to handle that level of attention in his personal life!'

Taylor, startled by the depth of her observations from such a small piece of information from forensics, immediately gathered his team and proceeded to inform them of her theories. He explained how all lone teenage girls in the area are potential next victims, due to the perpetrator's Modus Operandi.

Chapter II

Meanwhile, back at the Lee household, Georgie was absolutely correct, as a now elated Charles was secretly revelling in all the local and national media attention. On one hand he couldn't wait to get back out and find another girl to take, and indulge in a game of cat and mouse with the police. But on the other hand, he knew that they would be frantically searching for him, and he could not afford to make any potential mistakes. He thought on it for a moment and decided to wait for a couple of weeks until the publicity died down and see what developed in the meantime, and just continued to go about his everyday business as usual, even going as far as joining in prayers at church that weekend for the missing girls and the family of Amber Thompson.

It was now early March. Although Detective Taylor and his team, working alongside Miss Riley, were exploring a couple of leads and had brought in two men matching the profiling for questioning, they had no concrete evidence or definitive proof linking the men to the girls, or motive for that matter, and therefore had to release them, adding further frustration to the investigators.

The excitement was becoming too much for Charles to contain, as he thought to himself he had outwitted the police for a second time. He laughed at their incompetence in secret, and thought that now might be a good time to get back to the task at hand, and maybe help the police along the way. However, this time he would throw them a curveball; Mr Beattie would finally get his comeuppance, instead of a young girl — he was curious to see if Cumbria's finest in the constabulary could connect the dots.

***

Charles informed Rebecca the next day that he would be attending a business conference the following afternoon after work which would require him to be away for an overnight stay, as the conference was in Windermere in the heart of the Lake District. Although Rebecca thought this a tad unusual at such short notice, she never questioned her husband, as she knew he was doing all he could to make the practice successful and provide the family with a comfortable lifestyle. She just told Charles that she would miss him and asked him if there was anything in particular he needed to pack so she could prepare it for him. Charles informed her that everything was taken care of and he would only be needing an overnight bag, but thanked her anyway.

Charles woke bright and early the following morning, and after walking Tess then having breakfast, he kissed his two daughters on the cheeks before planting his lips on Rebecca's and gave her a long, lingering kiss. He instructed the children to behave for their mother, then told them he would see them all tomorrow. He exited the cottage then waved them goodbye, as he made his way to his car and drove away from the property.

Charles had a real sense of purpose about him this morning, and could not wait to get the formalities of work out of the way so he could concentrate solely on his preparations for his extracurricular indulgencies. Even Linda, his secretary, could sense that he had a spring in his step.

'What's made you so happy this morning, Charles?' she asked, as she made him his customary morning coffee.

'Lake District conference today!' he said happily, then explained to her how he would be leaving just before lunch, instructing her to pass over all his appointments for the afternoon to his colleagues.

Linda wasn't best pleased, as she knew the other vets wouldn't be very happy at having their workloads increased at such short notice, and knew she would end up taking the brunt of their frustrations, but she couldn't argue; again, resigning herself to the fact that he was the boss, after all.

Charles then took himself through to his office to contemplate tonight's events, and booked himself into a nice hotel in Windermere via his office computer to keep up appearances in case Rebecca was to question the truthfulness of what he had told her. As soon as it turned 11am Charles decided to leave the practice and make his way towards Windermere and check into his hotel room. He contemplated having a glass of wine whilst sitting out on the balcony that overlooked the beautiful and tranquil Lake Windermere, but stopped himself as he knew he had to remain one hundred percent level-headed and composed for what he had to do.

As evening drew ever nearer, Charles prepared a small rucksack to take with him which contained the remainder of the chloroform bottle, cable ties, surgical gloves, a small bottle of bleach, a length of rope, a balled gag with leather straps — the kind usually found in back street adult sex shops — a Stanley knife and, finally, a can of spray paint he had bought from a local hardware shop close to where he was staying. All he had to do now was wait until night arrived. He spent the remainder of the evening casually lying atop of his hotel bed, intently watching the twenty-four hour news channel, desperately hoping to catch a report of the on-going investigation. His mind raced over what would happen once the police discovered Jim's body, and if they would be competent enough to link the cases. He thought it was unlikely, so had a plan to leave them a very specific, but cryptic, clue to see if the psychological profiler he had seen on his TV screen alongside Detective Taylor was as smart as the police had portrayed her to be.

***

At 10.30pm, Charles decided he had waited long enough, and thought that Jim would probably be pouring vast quantities of whiskey down his neck before falling into an alcohol-fuelled slumber. Charles didn't bother to bring any ketamine along with him this night though, as he didn't want Jim to have the benefit of being unconscious when he got what was coming to him!

As he got into his Volvo and started the thirty-five to forty minute drive from Windermere to Haywood farm just outside of Wigton, he finally realised that he was now about to get the revenge he had desperately dreamed of all those years ago when he was a helpless young victim himself with nobody to protect him. His palms became increasingly sweaty and his heart raced faster the closer he came to the farm. He drove just below the speed limit all the way there, so as not to draw any attention to himself. He finally pulled up in a quiet country lane, the kind that only locals and farmers alike would know of, switched off his engine and exited the vehicle, shouldering his rucksack.

Charles stealthily made his way through private fields for nearly a mile before he found himself on the acres of land that surround the secluded Haywood farm. He gradually crept up towards the rear of the farmhouse, crouching so as not to be spotted as he approached ever closer. He spotted a light coming through the corridor from the front — it seemed like Jim might possibly still be awake — so he trod carefully, slowly pulling on the surgical gloves. He checked to see if he could prise open one of the dining room windows, to no avail. Gingerly, he made his way towards the back door and was shocked to find it unlocked; he gently pushed down on the handle, pausing for a second as the old wooden door creaked, then swiftly slid through the opening. Slowly and quietly, he closed the door behind him, turning the key in the lock.

His adrenaline now surged throughout his body as he removed the chloroform from his bag and filled his handkerchief once again, creeping along the hallway towards where the light was coming from in the sitting room. As he peered around the door leading into the sitting room, he could clearly make out an empty whiskey bottle laid out in front of an old armchair; Jim slumped, intoxicated, upon the armchair. Charles began to relax slightly and placed the handkerchief back inside his pocket; when Jim was in this state, it would take some considerable effort to wake him up.

With Jim passed out, Charles casually sauntered to the front door of the building to ensure it was also locked. Charles knew exactly what he had in store for Jim. He made his way back to the door he entered through and removed the keys, as he knew that Jim always kept the key to his gun cabinet alongside his house keys. Charles then made his way back through to the sitting room, turned the TV up slightly to drown out any screams, then approached the unconscious Jim. Smiling slightly, he started to remove Jim's clothing as he slept.

The old man stirred slightly as Charles began to remove his trousers and underwear. He called out for Edna whilst still asleep; for a split second, Charles began to pity the naked, sweaty, fat old man sleeping in front of him. The pity wasn't to last though, as he remembered exactly why he was here, and what Jim had subjected him to.

Charles again went into his bag and removed the industrial strength cable ties and placed a couple around Jim's ankles, binding them shut, then did the same to his wrists. Still, Jim did not wake. It wasn't until Charles placed the balled gag inside of Jim's mouth and pulled the strap hard as he tied it behind his head that Jim woke up in a state of shock and panic. He then desperately tried to make sense of what was happening but found it difficult to focus due to the vast amount of alcohol in his system. All he really knew was that there was a very serious possibility of something terrible happening to him.

Charles then dragged Jim to his feet from his seat with one mighty yank, and walked him towards the large coffee table that sat in the centre of the room. Charles instructed Jim to get down on his knees, stretch his arms out in front of him and bend over the table. He removed the rope and tied it through Jim's trembling wrists, then connected the other end to the radiator on the wall in front of him. Charles then viciously severed the back of Jim's ankles with the Stanley blade, cutting right through his Achilles tendons in doing so to make sure he couldn't get back to his feet. Jim tried to scream in agony, but his terror was muffled due to the gag in his mouth. Through the horrendous pain and shock he was in, Jim desperately tried to figure out just why the man he had invited into his home for coffee just a few months previously was doing this to him, but he was at a loss and could not understand what was happening.

Charles could sense that he was still unaware of his true identity. Sneering, he said, 'Let's see if this jogs your memory, eh, Jim?'

He took out the can of paint, removed the mirror that hung from the middle of the wall and started to write.

If a man also lie with mankind, as he lieth with a woman, both of them have committed an abomination: they shall surely be put to death; their blood shall be upon them.

Jim looked up at what he had written and immediately recognised it as a verse from the Bible, but still couldn't place Charles' face. However, he also knew in that instance that it must be one of the victims of his abuse.

'Now, don't you go anywhere!' Charles said sarcastically, and let him ponder over the Bible passage as he made his way out of the sitting room door and towards the stairs.

As he made his way up the stairs he grinned, as he could hear Jim whimpering and trying to free himself in desperation. Charles knew he wasn't going anywhere and took his time searching for the locked cabinet that contained Jim's licensed shotguns. He finally found it in the master bedroom and took the keys from his pocket and proceeded to unlock it. His eyes lit up as he discovered two firearms: one was a high calibre hunting rifle that he just passed right by, the other one, however, a single barrel shotgun. He picked the shotgun up and admired it wistfully. He then took a couple of cartridges from the box beside them and loaded one into the chamber.

As he made his way back down the stairs and towards the awaiting Jim, he noticed a thick, brass buckled belt hanging over a chair sat beside the door and decided he would put that to use also. Suddenly he couldn't help but wonder what Detective Taylor and the psychological profiler Georgina Riley would think once they discovered his latest work, and how they would view the man they were searching for.

Jim was totally slumped over on the table as Charles made his way back into the sitting room, in a kind of acceptance of the fate that was about to befall him. Charles placed the gun on the sofa, just out of arms reach of Jim but just close enough so he could see it, as if to rub salt into already stinging wounds, in a manner that suggested, 'if you can get it then you can gain your freedom' — but Charles knew it was a fruitless opportunity.

He then raised the belt aloft in his right hand and softly asked Jim, 'How about now, you sick fucking bastard!'

Before Jim even had time to think, Charles brought the thick buckle down upon the bare backside of Jim with one almighty swing that sent waves of excruciating pain throughout the old man's body. Lash after lash was delivered in a crazed frenzy, every one of them reminding him of the first time Mr Beattie had done it to him as an innocent, petrified schoolboy. This just spurred him on even more, and Jim's backside and lower back were covered in severe welts and blood by the time Charles regained his composure and relented what he was doing.

He put down the belt and approached Jim from the front; he noticed that Jim's face was completely tearstained and he appeared to be on the verge of passing out due to the sustained torture his body was being subjected to.

'DON'T YOU FUCKING DARE PASS OUT, YOU DISGUSTING PIECE OF SHIT! I HAVEN'T FUCKING FINISHED WITH YOU YET!'

He spat at the vile paedophile in front of him. Charles then lowered himself down to Jim's level of vision and looked him dead in the eye.

'Take a closer look, Jim, and tell me who you see.'

Charles held his gaze as Jim racked his brain trying to figure out who the man actually was that stood in front of him. After a few moments Charles saw in his eyes a moment of recognition and at that point he removed the gag from Jim's mouth so he could speak.

'No, no, it can't be. Jonathon?' he asked, desperately hoping he was wrong.

'And finally, the penny drops!' Charles snarled.

Jim frantically tried to apologise and reassure Charles that he had repented for his sins in a vain attempt to make him stop whatever it was he is about to do to him.

'Save your apologies, old man. The time has passed for that, now the time for retribution is upon you at the hands of the man whose life you ruined at a time when I needed you the most. I want you to know that I am going to enjoy every last minute of condemning your soul to hell!'

Charles then picked up the shotgun beside him and once again Jim pleaded for his life. His pleas fell on deaf ears. Jim then tried to scream for help, but this just made Charles laugh as he aimed the gun towards Jim's face and teasingly waved it in front of him.

'Open your fucking mouth,' Charles ordered. Jim hesitated, and Charles repeated more forcefully, 'I said open your fucking mouth, or I will blow your head off right now!'

This time he did as he was told.

Charles then placed the barrel into Jim's mouth and ordered him to suck it. He then repeated the words he had been told the very first time Jim had forced him to perform oral sex on him.

'Don't you dare try biting or screaming,' he said, 'because if you do, I will break your skinny little neck and bury you in the garden!'

He then forced the barrel deeper into his mouth, pushing it towards the back of his throat until it finally made him vomit. As Jim was throwing up, Charles smiled at him.

'Look at yourself you pathetic coward. Not very nice is it, Jim?'

All Jim could do was offer apology after apology but Charles had heard enough. It was time to put an end to this, he thought, then placed the gag that was hanging from Jim's neck back into his mouth once he had finished throwing up. He then made his way back towards Jim's heavily bleeding backside.

'Now for the finale, Jimmy boy,' he said maliciously. 'Hold on tight, because I have a feeling this might hurt you ever so slightly!'

With that, he forcefully rammed the saliva and vomit soaked barrel deep into Jim's rectum then proceeded to violate the beast of a man as he had done to him, totally removing any last bit of dignity Jim might have held.

Once he had humiliated him enough, not to mention the internal damage he had caused, he offered his final statement to his abuser and calmly said to him, 'You reap what you sow, old man. Tell Satan it was a messenger of God that sent you.'

Charles gently squeezed the trigger, and with an almighty bang, the shot-filled cartridge was dispatched into Jim's rectal passage and ripped right through his intestines and midriff, killing him instantly. Charles stood frozen to the spot for a few moments, his face totally covered in blood and faecal matter from the back draft of the force. His eyes were wide and his heart raced, then suddenly he was brought to his senses as the stench of human faeces filled his nostrils as Jim's bowels loosened and excrement oozed out of the gaping hole which was once his back passage. Charles was just about to grab his things and leave in case anybody had happened to hear the gun shot, but he paused to further desecrate Jim's body by taking out his Stanley knife from his pocket, slicing off Jim's penis, and placing it inside his mouth before repositioning the gag back in his mouth so it wouldn't fall out.

Charles stood back and proudly looked over his work for a few moments before gathering the remainder of his things and making his way towards the back door. He happened to catch a reflection of himself in a mirror that hung on the wall and made sure to wipe his face with a towel he found in the kitchen before he left, cleverly placing it inside his rucksack once he had used it so not to leave any DNA evidence at the murder scene.

He couldn't get away quickly enough as he

cautiously made his way back to his car, pulled out of the lane and approached the main road, but once again he regained composure and dropped down to the speed limit — especially now as it was after 2am and there weren't many cars on the road. Charles was on tenterhooks all the way back to Windermere, trying to avoid drawing any kind of suspicion to himself and couldn't wait to get out of the car and into the safety and comfort of his hotel room. He let out a huge sigh of relief as he pulled into the hotel car park and exited the vehicle as he knew he had made it back safely, and immediately went to his room to get cleaned up.

***

Charles never really slept that night as his tormented mind was overwhelmed with different emotions. He was happy to have finally orchestrated the ultimate revenge on the main perpetrator of his sustained abuse, but it also made him think back to the reasons for him ending up in the care system in the first place, specifically the deaths of Victoria and William McMullen, the only mum and dad he had ever known. He contemplated the life he would've had, and the person he would've became if life hadn't dealt him such a cruel blow.

This in turn led him to think of his birth mother: the figure of all his anger and frustrations, the reason for all his recent disgusting unlawful behaviours in his eyes. The reason that three young girls had lost their lives in the most horrific of circumstances. In the back of his mind he desperately wanted to find her and get answers to his many questions, but on the other hand he despised her for abandoning him to the life he had to endure.

He suddenly broke down in tears when the reality of his actions over the past few months came to the forefront of his mind. In that instance, he thought of the disgusting paedophile he had just humiliated and murdered and, although he had never thought about what he had done to the three girls in the same way before, it just suddenly dawned on him that he was no better than Jim was; life had gone full circle — he, the abused, innocent child, had now became the abuser. This in turn made him think of his loving wife, Rebecca, and adoring children, Molly and Fiona. The children, especially, would be absolutely disgusted and ashamed of their father if any of this was ever to emerge.

All he could do was sob as he thought to himself — how could he have been so stupid? He realised he would lose everything he held dear if he was to be caught. He contemplated taking his own life in his hotel room so none of his family members would be traumatised if they were to discover him. He did not know which way to turn, and just fell to his knees and prayed to God for forgiveness through tear-soaked eyes. His voice trembled as he swore he would never harm another young girl as he begged the Lord for forgiveness.

Chapter 12

As an exhausted Charles made his way to the practice the next morning, he wondered if Jim's body was yet to be discovered. He did not feel any remorse for what he had done to him, he just started to panic in case he had left any evidence that would connect him to the crime and bring his life crashing down. He frantically scanned the local radio stations but heard nothing of it as he pulled up outside of work.

The seconds felt like minutes, and minutes like hours that day, as Charles set about his daily tasks, eventually telling Linda that he was yet again finishing early as he wasn't feeling well. For the first time in a long time he just wanted to be home from work for his daughters arriving home from school; he desperately wanted to spend some time with them since last night's revelations had made him contemplate a life without them.

Rebecca was taken aback and thought it odd as he surprised her by making his way into the family home just after 2pm in the afternoon. She was even more surprised as he scooped her up in his arms without saying a word, and proceeded to carry her to the bedroom and gently laid her on the bed.

'Stop, what are you doing, mister?' she said feebly, trying to understand where this behaviour was coming from.

Still silent, he planted his lips onto hers and passionately kissed her, in doing so, letting her know exactly what he had in mind. Rebecca looked at the clock and realised it would be a good hour or so before the girls were due to arrive home off the school bus, and decided to just go along with it and kissed him back ardently. There were to be no twisted delusions or any clasping of her neck this time though; no, this time he made love to his wife and upon finishing, held her in a loving embrace, one that he never wanted to end. He cursed himself again. How had he been so stupid to risk losing the woman and family he loved?

They lay there for a while in each other's embrace, before eventually getting up and dressed just in time for the girls returning from school. Charles then spent the next few hours actively playing and engaging with his children as he used to. He even made extra efforts to communicate on a more adult level with his eldest daughter, Molly, whom he had recently lost a connection with, as he hated the thought of her turning into a young lady and possibly ending up like his birth mother. He put that thought to the back of his mind though, as he just wanted to enjoy spending time with his family, and decided in that instance to tell Rebecca and the children that he was going to be handing over more responsibilities to his colleagues as of now, therefore freeing up more time to be at home with them. The girls let out a 'YAY' in unison, and Rebecca smiled; she'd missed having her husband around more often.

***

Meanwhile, there was a hive of activity down on Haywood farm, as a concerned neighbour from a nearby farm thought it a bit odd at not seeing Jim out tending to his cattle this day, and had decided to go and give the man a knock and see if all was ok earlier that afternoon. As he approached he noticed that Jim's Land Rover was parked around the side of the building near to the barn, and decided to check the back door as he started to become concerned for the old man. Once again there was no answer. He thought this very strange, and also wondered as to why the curtains in the front room were still closed so late in the day. The concerned farmer decided to try knocking one last time on the front door before trying to get a glimpse through the sitting room curtains. He was to get the shock of his life as he did so; through a thin crack in the curtains, he could clearly make out the naked, blood-soaked body of Jim, bound and gagged and slumped over the coffee table. He reeled in horror as the reality of what he had just seen registered in his mind. Through shock and terror he finally managed to remove his mobile phone from his pocket with trembling hands and dialled 999.

***

A junior CID member was speaking to his senior officer, Detective Taylor, who was busy discussing potential motives as to the three girls' disappearance with his temporary partner during this case, Miss Georgina Riley.

'You're not going to believe this, guv.'

'What's that?' Taylor asked.

'Well sir, it's probably nothing to do with what you're working on, but we've just received a call from a farmer near Wigton informing us that he has just discovered the body of his neighbour.'

'And what the hell has that got to do with me?' Taylor angrily snapped back at his colleague. 'Can't you see we are busy?' He turned his back on his junior.

'It's just —'

'IT'S JUST WHAT?'

'Well sir,' the junior detective said timidly, 'from what I could gather through the man's shaky voice, he thinks that his neighbour has been murdered. But more specifically, he said he could make out the deceased man's hands were bound with cable ties, and it just made me think of the girl that was dragged from the river, Amber Thompson.'

This got Taylor's attention. He turned and looked questioningly at Georgie.

'It might be unrelated,' she said, 'but I think we should maybe go check it out, don't you?'

Taylor agreed and sheepishly thanked his junior that he had just berated for the good work.

***

By the time they reached Haywood farm there was already a team of local police officers there, taping off entry to the crime scene. As the detective showed his badge, one of the officers who was first at the scene spoke to Taylor.

'Sir, I must warn you. In all my time on the force I have never seen anything like what you are about to witness in there.'

Taylor shrugged it off and proceeded past the officer, with Georgie following closely behind. The first thing they both noticed was the stench as it attacked their nostrils the moment they entered the property. Neither of them were prepared for what they were about to witness next as they made their way into the sitting room and laid their eyes over the gruesome image that confronted them, not before noticing the words daubed across the wall in thick, black lettered paint. Taylor did his best in offering comfort to Georgie who was clearly distressed at what she was seeing. But unbeknown to her, Taylor was also struggling to take in this crime scene, as it was unlike anything he had ever seen before.

He immediately spoke to the few other officers in the room and told them not to touch anything until the forensic team arrived, as he didn't want the crime scene being contaminated. As Taylor inspected the dead man sprawled atop of the coffee table, he paid special attention to the cable ties the neighbour who had reported it had mentioned, and realised that they were bound together in the exact same fashion as the ones found on Amber's wrists and ankles, with two placed around both the limbs, and one tied in between to draw them in even tighter and drastically reduce the chance of escape.

'What do you make of that?' he asked Georgie as he pointed to the man's wrists.

'It certainly looks the same as the ones found on Amber's body, but something just doesn't add up.'

'In what way?'

'Well for a start, without stating the obvious, why would our guy change tact and all of a sudden target old men, for example? And secondly, why would he start leaving us clues or signs, when he has been so careful to avoid detection thus far?'

'Beats me!' Taylor admitted. 'But I know one thing, whoever it is that is capable of doing something like this is one seriously fucked up individual.'

Georgie left Taylor to continue to inspect the mess that was once Jim's body, and fixed her eyes firmly on the wall beside him. As she read the passage over and over again, she desperately tried to make sense of the message. What was he trying to tell them? She racked her brain, trying to make sense of it all.

Taylor could see that she was clearly perplexed by the writing on the wall. 'Do you think this could be a spurned gay lover's act of revenge?'

Georgie rolled her eyes and looked at him as though he was an uneducated oaf. 'Take a look around you and tell me what you see?'

Taylor was lost and asked her to be more specific.

'Well I don't know if you have noticed, but all around us are pictures of the victim and what I can only presume to be his wife. And judging by the fact that the pictures appear to span over a long time period, and the fact that she isn't here right now, would suggest to me that maybe she is no longer with us.'

An embarrassed Taylor again did not have a

response, but didn't let her condescending tone faze him; he knew she was smarter than him and, if truth be told, this just added to his attraction to her. 'So what is your theory on the message?' he asked.

'I'm not quite sure just yet, but I am pretty certain that we need to speak to somebody from the Christian church, as this is definitely a biblical quote, I'm just not one hundred per cent sure as to the motive.'

***

As the pair of them prepared to leave the farm in the hands of the arriving forensic team, Taylor can't help but notice that the dead man he now knows as Mr James Beattie appeared to have bulging cheeks — and not just from the gag which was pushed to the front of his mouth. He leant down to take a closer look and took out a pen from his jacket pocket with his gloved hand. Slowly, carefully, he placed the pen in the man's mouth to try to prise open his jaw and gain an insight as to what it may contain. As the mouth opened, the detective reeled back in horror as the man's once-attached genitalia flopped out and dropped onto the floor in front of him. All he could do is cover his mouth with his hand; this was unlike anything he had ever witnessed before. He swiftly stood upright and passed over this information to the forensic experts before he and Georgie made their way out of the house, towards their waiting car. Taylor spoke only to tell one of the police officers outside to get a full, detailed statement from the neighbour who had made the call, and also instructed them to knock on all the surrounding properties and find out if anybody had witnessed anything.

***

As they pulled away from the farm and made their way back towards Carlisle, Taylor turned to Georgie.

'I sure could do with a drink after seeing that! Care to join me?'

She too needed a drink and somewhere to sit and ponder over what had just occurred, at least to try and figure out what it all meant and, more importantly, what led to Mr Beattie's gruesome end.

She nodded. 'Sure, it might do us both some good.'

Taylor then took his colleague back to the hotel where she was staying and parked the car, and both headed inside and towards the bar area.

Georgie asked Taylor, 'What will it be? I'll get these in'.

Taylor liked her more and more by the minute. 'I'll have a brandy please Georgie, and make it a large one would you?'

'Coming right up,' she informed him.

She casually strolled towards the bar, leaving Taylor to find somewhere for them to sit. He couldn't help but cast his eyes over her slender frame and pert behind as he watched her approach the bar.

He pulled out his phone and proceeded to send his wife a text message informing her that he might not be home till late this evening, as a new lead had come up at work. All lies, of course. He had always fancied himself as a bit of a womaniser, and had already indulged in a number of pre-marital affairs behind his wife's back; he was hoping tonight may lead to something happening between him and the beautiful new colleague assigned to him, as he was convinced he had sensed a chemistry between them.

He quickly put the phone away as she made her return from the bar with their drinks. She lounged back into her chair with a sigh, mentally drained after such an intense day, her head spinning.

The pair of them sat for the next couple of hours drinking and engaging in general conversation, anything to try and get their minds off the day's events, and spoke about trivial and mundane things instead.

The later it became, and the more the drink flowed, the conversation inevitably became more relaxed and now relatively loosened due to the alcohol consumption, the topic of sex came up when Georgie asked about his wife. Taylor palmed her off with some half-arsed story about him and his wife drifting apart and only staying together out of habit, and that it was a loveless marriage.

'I'm more interested as to why such an intelligent, beautiful, young woman like you is still single...?'

Georgie blushed at his flattery and thanked him for his kind words, placing her hand on his as she did so. Her touch lingered just that little bit too long, deliberately giving him the green light to continue, as she too had started to develop an attraction to him. Even though she knew it was wrong as he was a married man, and it went against her morals, she had a weakness for men in authority; even though she sometimes didn't like his arrogance, she could not help but find his commitment and drive a turn on.

Taylor didn't need any further encouragement and thought it was time to flirtatiously test the water. 'Well, I suppose I'd better be making my way home and let you get your beauty sleep — not that you need it, I might add.'

He pulled his car keys out of his pocket.

'You aren't in any fit state to be driving anywhere tonight, mister!' she fired back at him, then playfully snatched the keys from his hand.

By this point he knew his cunning plan had worked and was just waiting for her to offer her bed for the night. 'Well, what else do you suggest?' he asked coyly.

'Well,' she says, 'there is option A, where you could call a cab and I will bring your car into work tomorrow, which could potentially pose some questions and suspicious looks. Or, there is option B.'

'Which is?' he asked her before she even had chance to finish what she was saying.

'We could stay down here and have another couple of drinks and put the world to rights, but seeing as it looks as though the bar staff are gearing up to close for the night, we could grab a bottle of wine or two, and maybe head up to my room for a night cap before you book into one of the other rooms for the night. What do you reckon?'

He thought about this for a few seconds, trying to figure out how he would explain it to his wife, then decided to take her up on her offer. Excusing himself, he left for the bathroom and rang his wife to inform her that he won't be home at all now, as he and his team would be working through the night to try and solve the case. She knew this case was the biggest of his career so decided not to question him, even though she knew he was probably lying; she had just kind of accepted her husband for the man that he was, choosing to live in blissful ignorance rather than face the truth.

Upon his return, Georgie flashed him a smile as she raised her hands, showing him she had already got the wine, then led him to her room. They both knew what was going to happen as they staggered and swayed along the corridor and up the stairs towards where she was staying, but in an alcohol fuelled state they couldn't see past their lust and think how it may affect their professional relationship. They had barely finished their first glass of wine in the room before they were tearing off each other's clothes and making passionate love to one another, totally lost in the euphoria of the moment. Taylor never did book into another room that night, as by the time they had finished they had both fell asleep in her bed in a sweaty mess, totally exhausted.

***

Georgie was the first to wake early the following morning; her head was pounding from the effects of the alcohol and she was blurry eyed due to lack of sleep. God, please let it all have been a dream. She nervously rolled over and freaked out when she saw Taylor still fast asleep beside her. She then peeked under the duvet; her thoughts of last night's events were confirmed when she saw that they were both still fully undressed.

She made her way out of the bed and towards the bathroom, picking her way through the numerous items of clothing strewn across the hotel room floor. As she closed the bathroom door behind her, she sat on the toilet with her head held in her hands. What had she done? She could not believe that she had potentially destroyed a marriage, and promised herself that she would not let anything like this ever happen again. She stepped into the shower and cleansed herself of any evidence of last night's actions ever taking place.

Back in the bedroom, Taylor was also starting to regain his senses and, although he felt guilty for deceiving his wife, he'd actually really enjoyed the previous night and hoped it may develop into something more regular. He was taken aback as Georgie returned from the bathroom draped only in a towel that wrapped around her slender frame, with her hair still soaking wet and dripping down her front as she picked up a brush and started to run it through her sodden locks. Taylor glanced up at her sheepishly; as his eyes met hers he could tell that she was remorseful as she immediately disengaged from his gaze and looked at the floor.

'Last night should never have happened,' she said firmly. 'I don't know what came over me. You are married and I feel like a complete and utter bitch! Please can we forget that last night ever happened and get back to being just colleagues? I don't want this to affect our working relationship.'

Taylor could sense her genuine sincerity and remorse and, although he was somewhat disappointed, he agreed. He scooped up his underwear from beside the bed and made his way past Georgie and towards the bathroom to shower himself.

***

The pair of them made their separate ways to work that morning so as to avoid any awkward questioning or suspicion. They simply nodded knowingly at each other and greeted each other with a 'good morning' as they met at the headquarters of the investigation.

Taylor rallied his team together to see if any more information had come to light in the wake of Mr Beattie's murder, and also in the investigation into the three girls. He addressed his team.

'Right, this is what we know. Due to yesterday's discovery, it is looking very much a possibility that the case with the dead farmer, Mr Beattie, and the case of Amber Thompson may possibly be related due to the exact same way in which their limbs were bound together. Although the M.O. does not match up with the previous three girls' disappearances, it is looking as though we are faced with the very real possibility that this is the work of a serial killer. And the likelihood is that he *will* strike again.'

He paused for effect as members of the team around him shuffled uncomfortably.

'I want to know everything there is to know about James Beattie — anything that might give us some indication of why he was brutally killed. His lifestyle, his family, his friends, anything that can maybe shed some light on why he could have become the victim. And as far as the press, or anybody else for that matter, is concerned, we are investigating the two cases separately and there is no obvious connection between them. The last thing we need is more nationwide media coverage and speculation over the issue, and not to mention mass hysteria in the local community if they were to believe that a serial killer is on the loose!'

Taylor dismissed his staff, letting them return to what they had been previously been doing. He then looked at Georgie.

'You come with me.'

Chapter 13

There was an awkward silence between the two of them as they made their way downstairs and out into the car park towards Taylor's waiting car. As they entered the vehicle, Taylor just had to get the elephant out of the room and assured Georgie that he wholeheartedly agreed with what she had told him earlier. He was lying, of course, as he undoubtedly wanted a repeat performance, but did not want her to resign her services as he knew he was much more likely to solve the case with her expertise. She could see right through his comments but just chose to nod in agreement and assured him that from now on until the case is over she would conduct herself professionally at all times. The pair of them finally became more relaxed.

'Where are you taking me?' Georgie asked.

'We're going to see Minister Davies from Carlisle Cathedral to try and get an understanding of the meaning behind the message the killer left for us on the wall at the murder scene. He has agreed to meet with us this morning to try and assist us with any of our questions.'

She agreed that this was probably a good idea, and they left the station car park and made their way to see the minister. When they arrived they were greeted by the clergyman. Details of James Beattie's murder were yet to be released to the press, so Minister Davies had no idea why the detective and his colleague had arranged to meet with him; all Taylor had told him over the phone was that he needed some help deciphering a biblical verse and its meaning. The minister welcomed the two of them into his private chambers, offered them a seat and exchanged pleasantries. Finally, they got down to business.

'So, what exactly can I do for you today?' the clergyman asked.

Taylor removed his notebook from his jacket pocket and opened it to the page where he had written down the quote word for word. 'Can you explain the meaning behind the words and where they came from?'

As Minister Davies read the words he knew instantly that they were from the King James Version of the Bible. It was a passage from Levictus 20:13. He just didn't know why they would bring it to him instead of just typing the verse into a search engine to find the source and meaning.

His curiosity was now excited and he couldn't help himself from asking, 'What is this in relation to, Detective?'

'Would it make a difference?' Taylor replied.

The minister knew full well that he is not being given the full picture. 'Well, actually, it would make a massive difference if it was taken out of context! What I mean by that is that first and foremost this is a direct quote from the Bible, more specifically the King James Version, which in itself has more of a hellfire and damnation feel about it. Secondly, you would not be bringing this to me just to explain this to you unless it was directly related to something I may be able to help you with.'

'For example?' Taylor asked.

The minister was extremely confident now that the detective wasn't being exactly forthright with him. 'Proof-texting by any chance?' he said, in a manner that showed Taylor that he had a fairly good idea of why he had arranged to meet with him.

Taylor was unfamiliar with this term, but before

he could ask the minister to elaborate, Georgie quickly chirped in.

'Oh yes, of course! The art of taking verses and passages from the Bible and twisting the meanings to suit yourself, or something along those lines. Why didn't I think of that? We learnt about that in our third year of study at university. I can't believe I didn't remember.'

She knew exactly why she hadn't remembered, and that it was because she had been riddled with guilt all morning thinking about what had happened the night before, but now it was all starting to make sense.

'You're almost right,' the minister says to Georgie.

'Almost?' Taylor asked.

'Proof-texting, Detective. It is the habit of taking verses out of the Bible, out of context, and forcing your ideas onto the text. For example, you could say that the Bible says that "*there is no god*", because it does say that, but only if you take that phrase out of context of the verse in the book of Psalms. Psalms 10:4 to be exact. In it, it says "*In the pride of his face the wicked does not seek him; all his thoughts are, there is no god*".'

Minister Davies looked at the detective and could see that he wasn't quite grasping what he was telling him, and went on. 'Let me tell you about a humorous proof-texting experience that apparently happened when a man was desperate for God to speak to him over a situation he found himself in. The man opened the Bible at a random place and read Mathew 27:5 which talked about Judas, who betrayed Jesus and then went and hanged himself. The man thought that this was a bit odd, but went again and randomly opened it at Luke 10:37, and Jesus said to him, "*You go and do likewise*".

'You see, Detective, the point I am trying to make is that two different people can look at and read the very same material, yet have two totally different opinions of the meaning of what they have read. And by taking it out of context, they can make it fit to whatever situation they find themselves in. With that in mind, it would probably be beneficial for you to explain to me your reason for being here, so that I may be able to help you.'

Taylor, by this point, was in total agreement and decided to entrust the minister with the information and circumstances surrounding Mr Beattie's murder. He told the clergyman the events at length.

'Given the details of what you have just told me, Detective, and the way in which Mr Beattie was killed, and the fact that the Levictus quote was found beside the body, suggests that this was the act of a man. Obvious, I know, but what do we know of Mr Beattie? Was he a homosexual man?'

Georgie once again rolled her eyes as Taylor flashed her a smug smile, as he had been totally shot down by her the previous night when he dared to question the sexuality of Mr Beattie.

'He was a married man for many years and a well-respected member of the local community by all accounts,' Georgie explained respectfully.

Minister Davies seemed somewhat puzzled and further probed, 'Are you one hundred per cent sure of this? As this statement would clearly suggest otherwise! What else can you tell me of the man?'

'Well, according to research conducted since yesterday, it would appear that he and his wife were practising Christians and regularly attended church, and they were also very much involved in charity work in the community. They didn't have any children of their own, but apparently they were long-term foster parents for children throughout Cumbria for a period of about twenty-five years.'

'Interesting...'

'What do you mean?' Taylor asked, intrigued.

'Does Mr Beattie have any kind of criminal record on file?' the minister probed.

'There was an arrest and caution for a domestic disturbance in the early 80s, and also again a couple of years later for another drunken disturbance in the home, but no charges were ever brought against him as his wife would never give evidence against her husband according to our archives.'

Davies thought for a second before asking one last question. 'And what about any sexual offences detective?'

'Absolutely nothing, like I said, the man was practically faultless in the eyes of the law.'

'I suggest you dig a little deeper, Detective, because I believe that whoever did this — and like I say, the verse suggests it was the actions of a man — inflicted this torture and death on Mr Beattie in a revenge attack. His actions were either that of a spurned lover or perhaps the actions of someone who was the victim of abuse at Mr Beattie's hands.

'I would suggest you start by going over the records of all the young people he and his wife fostered and see if you can find any evidence to back up this suggestion, and maybe try and locate the people you find on that list. As I believe that somewhere in this you will find your answers'. Taylor and Georgie then thanked the minister for his time before leaving the Cathedral and making their way back towards the car. Davies followed them to the door before adding one last comment. 'Find the victims Detective, and I guarantee you will find the killer!'

Back at the car, Taylor turned to Georgie.

'What did you make of all that?'

'It makes perfect sense in my eyes' she reluctantly replied, as she realised she had totally overlooked this angle of enquiries.

***

Back at the station, Taylor left it to Georgie to relay

this information to the team and to try and get a list of all the children that were looked after by the Beatties in all their years as foster carers. In the meantime, he went to see his senior, Chief Inspector Ian Messenger. As Taylor relayed all the new theories to the Chief Inspector, he could clearly see that his senior was becoming more uncomfortable with what he was hearing.

'Everything okay, sir?'

'No, no, everything is not okay, Detective Taylor! I've got the case of the three girls casting a shadow over this station, with people wanting answers. Now there's been another murder in the shape of James Beattie. You are suggesting that this is possibly some sort of revenge attack for some kind of abuse that happened years ago. You're telling me that these cases are related and there is potentially a serial killer at large in our community. That's not to mention the media circus that swarms outside the station every day, so you can pretty much rest assured that everything is not o-fucking-kay!

'I want some fucking answers, and I want them fast, as I now have to go and give another statement to the press and inform them about the death of Mr fucking Beattie, and once again I do not have anything concrete to give them. And another thing, Taylor...'

'Yes, sir?'

'I want kept up to date on any further developments in both cases as soon as anything — and I mean *anything* — arises, you hear me?'

'Yes, sir.'

Taylor left from Chief Inspector Messenger's office and back towards his team and Georgie.

'Right guys, shit just got serious. I gather Miss Riley here has informed you all of the new information regarding the death of James Beattie? I want a list of all the kids that the Beatties have ever fostered over the years, and I want them yesterday. Now everybody get back to work and find me something I can use!'

With that, everyone went back to their desks to try to gather information for their boss. Detective Taylor headed to his office, slamming the door behind him as he entered, his pride dented after the berating he had just received from Messenger.

Chapter 14

Family life seemed back to normal in the Lee household; Rebecca and the children were enjoying having Charles around more over the last few days and the family was really starting to reconnect — so much so that Charles hadn't even bothered to follow the recent news as he had done before. Instead he chose to concentrate on odd jobs around the home he had put off as of late, therefore trying not to give thought to what he had done over the past few months. He thought he was starting to turn over a new leaf and put it all behind him, totally resisting his narcissistic urge to play with and torment the police and their enquiries.

***

The media didn't go public with the news of Mr Beattie's murder until a few days after Chief Inspector Ian Messenger's meeting with the press, as he had asked them for a couple of days grace whilst his detectives determined whether or not the cases were related before they released the details of the old man's death. He knew that when the news went public, and if the horrific details in which he was murdered were to emerge, the media circus would just increase tenfold, and the added pressure could hinder his officers in their investigations.

He soon received the post mortem verdict on Jim Beattie, accompanied by the forensic report. The report stated that the cable ties used were the exact same type and batch as those used on Amber Thompson — plus the fact that they were tied in the exact same way — thus confirming his suspicions that the cases were connected. Chief Inspector Messenger, after much pressure from his superiors and the victim's families, reluctantly contacted the media yet again to confirm the findings.

***

Charles and Rebecca had not long sat down on the sofa after cleaning up following their evening meal when all of a sudden the programme they were watching was interrupted. In its place was an incoming news bulletin, headed by Chief Inspector Ian Messenger.

'It is with great sadness that I can now confirm that there is a direct link between the murders of Mr James Beattie and Amber Thompson. At this point we also strongly believe that the person responsible for these two crimes is responsible for the disappearances of the two missing schoolgirls, Lucy Mitchell and Sarah Davidson. This is now a direct plea to the person responsible to come forward and give themselves up and put an end to this matter. If you come forward and cooperate now, it will be a better outcome for all involved.'

Messenger ended his address by finally reassuring the public that his dedicated team was following several leads, determined to bring the investigations to a swift end.

Charles felt sick to the pit of his stomach at what he had just seen. Not because the police had actually connected the dots and knew they were looking for the same person in connection to the cases; not even due to the fact that the news made him think about the girls he had abused and murdered, and the promise he had made to never hurt another. No, what made him feel sick this time in was that he actually believed he recognised the man on his TV screen.

No, it can't be.

The last time he had seen the man he was then just a junior police officer in his twenties back in the 80s. Charles searched deep into his memory to try and recollect the faces of all his abusers at that time — memories he had tried desperately to forget. But there was no denying it; Chief Inspector Ian Messenger was definitely one of the men that had not only visited Jim around that time, but he was also one of the men that frequented the terrified young boy's bedroom. This absolutely enraged Charles, who, sensing Rebecca was beginning to tell something wasn't right, decided he was going to take Tess for a walk to clear his head, as he needed some fresh air.

***

Charles followed any further developments with real intent over the following days and, after scanning through the many articles in the local and national papers, he finally came across the details he was looking for, confirming the time and date of the funeral of Mr James Beattie. In that moment he decided that he would go along, in an effort to see if not only Ian Messenger would attend, but to see if he recognised any of the other guests.

Charles sat and watched over the funeral proceedings through binoculars from his parked car, a fair distance from where the coffin was being hoisted down into the freshly dug grave. And just as he expected, he immediately spotted the Chief Inspector. He also recognised another face, one he hadn't given thought to for a very long time. It was that of his old Social worker, Brian. Although Brian had never actually physically abused him, he knew that the ex-Social worker knew all about Jim's ways and habits, and the atrocities that were committed at the farm, yet chose to do nothing to prevent it from happening, which in Charles' eyes made him just as guilty as Jim.

After the funeral proceedings had finished, Charles decided to follow the man and see where he would go to next. He followed him in his car all the way from Wigton to somewhere he had not been for a very long time — Whitehaven, the place in which he spent his earliest years, the place that held so many mixed emotions and memories for him. Charles barely recognised the place as he drove through it and onto the outskirts of town. He pulled up by the side of the road and sat and watched as a now portly old Brian pulled into his driveway and entered his house.

Got you, you bastard.

Charles smirked and pulled away, heading towards home.

Chapter 15

Back at police headquarters, Detective Taylor and his team, including Georgie, were working tirelessly, trying to contact the extensive list of names they had received from Social Services regarding the children that came and went from the Beattie household over the years.

As they tracked down one victim after another and questioned them over their stay with the Beattie's, a pattern started to emerge. Nearly every one of them explained how beatings and sexual abuse were the norm in the household at that time and that, although she wasn't a part of it, Edna knew it happened and chose to do nothing about it out of fear of her husband.

Apparently it wasn't just Mr Beattie who was part of the systematic abuse; many of the victims informed him and Georgie how they were often given alcohol and sometimes drugged before being passed around to many visiting men at that time. Taylor was shocked to hear how some of them mentioned that the police were involved also, and stopped many of them coming forward with their allegations. The one common denominator in the majority of the children being placed into the care of the Beattie's throughout that period seemed to be that most of them were referred there by one Social worker in particular, Mr Brian Jenkins. Detective Taylor decided that now would be a very good time to locate and speak with Mr Jenkins to find out exactly what he knew, and investigate his direct involvement with James Beattie at the time that this horrendous abuse was taking place.

***

Taylor turned and spoke to Georgie as they headed out of the station the following morning and made their way towards Whitehaven to speak with the ex-Social worker Brian Jenkins. 'I think the minister might be onto something.'

Georgie looked at him and nodded her head. 'It would appear so.'

She desperately hoped they may get some answers from Mr Jenkins as to why this abuse was allowed to happen, and also to see if he could point them in the right direction of who may be responsible for Jim's death. By this point, Taylor and Georgie had managed to forget about the night they spent together at the hotel, and were now concentrating solely on having a professional working relationship until this whole case had been resolved.

As they pulled up and knocked at Brian's house, they were greeted by him at the front door in a warm and pleasant manner. Brian informed them he would try and answer any questions they might have to the best of his knowledge, then added that what they had to remember was that it was a very long time ago so his memory may be a little hazy. Taylor, immediately sensing his evasiveness, got straight down to business and directly to the point.

'So, Mr Jenkins, tell me exactly in what context did you know the Beatties, and why was it that you referred so many young people into their care during your time with Social Services?'

'Well, Detective Taylor, is it? I will start by saying that I can assure you that the Beatties were thoroughly vetted before any children were placed in their care, and all manner of safeguarding measures were put in place by myself and my seniors to ensure the safety and wellbeing of the young people we cared for. As for my involvement with the family, I would regularly visit the farm to check on all the young people, who always appeared to be well looked after and nourished during their stay with the Beatties. May I ask what exactly has this got to do with Jim's death, Detective? You said on the phone that you wanted to speak with me regarding that matter.'

'Without going into too much detail, Mr Jenkins, fresh evidence has come to light in the wake of Mr Beattie's death regarding the happenings in the Beattie household over the years that would suggest that Jim was perhaps part of some sort of paedophile ring, and after speaking with numerous people who stayed with the Beatties over this period, many of them claim that they were subjected to serious sexual abuse and beatings.

'With that in mind, Brian — do you mind if I call you Brian? — this leads us to suspect that maybe one of these victims has resurfaced to exact revenge. I wondered if you could provide us with any information as to which one of the many children you looked after, so well I might add, and help us find this person before he goes looking for other people involved in the abuse?'

Brian's voice was shaky and broken as he replied. 'I hope you are not suggesting that I had anything to do with the abuse, Detective Taylor? Should I have a solicitor present right now?'

Georgie, who until now had sat quietly, decided to interject as she could tell Taylor had no time for this man, and strongly suspected that he knew far more than he is letting on. 'No, Mr Jenkins, that is not necessary. What Detective Taylor here is merely trying to establish is A, How well you knew the Beatties, and B, if you can shed any kind of light on any incidents you may be aware of as to who could have possibly committed Jim's murder, and possibly the reasons behind it so we can bring the perpetrator to justice?

'The thing is, Mr Jenkins, you obviously would have worked closely with the young people you looked after, and we were just wondering if you could possibly remember any incidents, no matter how insignificant you think it may be, that may trigger your memory. I understand it was a long time ago as you have already stated, but was there anyone or any particular incident whatsoever that you can think of that might lead us to something we can work with?'

Before Brian could speak, Taylor added, 'In other words Brian, is there anyone you looked after that you think could have wanted to come back and kill Mr Beattie?'

Brian sat and thought about what he had just been asked.

'No, nobody stands out.'

Just as Taylor and Georgie were about to get up and leave, Brian spoke up.

'Wait.'

Taylor and Georgie sat back down in their seats and awaited Brian's next words with baited breath.

'There was one incident I do recall, now I think about it.'

'Please, continue,' Georgie quickly followed up, in doing so not giving him time to concoct his story if he was making it up.

'Yes now I remember. There was an incident involving a young boy by the name of Jonathon McMullen, who I had to go and collect from the Beatties' farm one morning after he had beaten Jim in an apparently unprovoked attack.

'Yes, we have his name and are waiting to make contact with Jonathon McMullen soon hopefully, but at present we don't seem to be able to locate him, maybe you might be able to help us with this matter, Brian?' Taylor then asked.

'Oh, I haven't seen that young man since not long after that day, Detective Taylor, and to be honest with you I'm glad of that fact; if I remember correctly, he was an extremely disturbed young man with a bit of a temper. He also seemed to be a bit of a fantasist as well, often making up lies about the Beatties, and accused Jim of beating not only him, but his own wife Edna also.'

Brian knew straight away he had said too much, and quickly started to back pedal on what he had just said. But it was too late, as Taylor and Georgie picked up on it instantly.

'So, Mr Jenkins, what you are telling us is that you had a young person in your care who actually came forward and told you about the goings on in that household and you chose to do nothing. Is that what you are telling us?'

'Er, er, I mean, like I said to you before, we had no reason to suspect anything untoward was happening in the house, and they were extremely well vetted and respectable members of the community. They were God fearing, Christian churchgoers for heaven's sake, and we had no reason to doubt them.'

'So you simply chose to do nothing, and ignore the pleas of a desperate young boy,' Taylor snapped back. 'And in doing so, condemned many more children to the same fate!'

He then got up and made his way towards the front door, blood boiling from what he had just been told, with Georgie following closely behind. But before Taylor exited the house he offered one final comment to an extremely riled and shaken Brian.

'I hope for your sake that you had nothing to do with the abuse, because if I find out otherwise Brian, I will be coming back for you, and I will not be held responsible for my actions! Do you understand?'

All Brian could do was nod his head; he had been left speechless and petrified after what Taylor had just told him, as he knew he had meant every word of the threat he had just made.

'That was a bit unprofessional don't you think?' Georgie asked him as they made their way back to the car.

'Not at all,' he replied. 'I was just trying to scare

him to see what he does. I want a team put on him around the clock to see what he does next, because if he was a part of the network, it will be interesting to see who else he contacts from hereon in.'

Georgie hadn't thought about it this way, and started regaining admiration for the man she had been working closely with over the past month.

'Now, I want you to see exactly what you can find on Jonathon McMullen and the other few names we have been unable to make contact with on the list, Georgie. Concentrate mainly on Jonathon, as I think that might just throw something up, as Brian was reluctant to give us anything useful.'

'No problem, I'll get on to it as soon as we get back.'

***

With the search for Jonathon McMullen in full flow along with the other few remaining names on the list, Taylor strongly believed they were actually getting somewhere, but stuck with his instinct and placed another team of detectives on around the clock surveillance of Brian Jenkins, as he was convinced he was hiding information from him. He even went as far as getting a judge's permission to monitor all his phone and internet activity, as he knew it wasn't just the case of the three girls, or the murder of James Beattie; he was now starting to think even bigger than that. He thought he might even be able to bring down a paedophile ring that had had upper echelons in positions of authority for possibly the last thirty years, and he thought he could maybe expose these people that had remained hidden in plain sight for all that time. Taylor's mind was working overtime right now, and he had even started to distrust his own officers in his CID division and above, and urged his small team of officers to bring any new information directly to him and keep it "hush hush" — although he did not explain his reasons why.

No matter which way she turned, Georgie could not gather any information on Jonathon McMullen whatsoever since he left the care of the local authorities when he turned sixteen years old. It was as though he had just miraculously disappeared; there wasn't a single record of his existence after that time, and she was at a loss as to where to go from here. She had contemplated that he had possibly changed his name, but was told by staff at the deed poll department that they had no record of anybody by that name. Georgie just could not understand how a person could disappear without a trace; she had thought that maybe he had left the country, but that avenue of enquiries had also come back without success. She had nothing to offer Taylor that could help find his whereabouts.

The following week one of Taylor's staff brought him a list of all Brian Jenkins' phone calls from the past five days and handed it to him in his office. As he perused this new information, one of the numbers kept popping up day after day, sometimes numerous calls in a single twenty-four hour period. Taylor decided to get records on all of the numbers and was shocked at the list of names that showed up. There was a doctor, a magistrate, even a local MP, but none of that shocked him as much as the number that was dialled most frequently. He was rooted to the spot as he read the name in front of him: Mr Ian Messenger!

Taylor quickly whipped out his phone and double-checked the number; he was saddened to see that the number matched the one he had for his Chief Inspector. Right at that very moment Chief Inspector Messenger appeared, and was keen to get an update on any recent developments in the case.

'Well sir, we have managed to track down the majority of the people who were looked after by the Beatties, and they all seem to be giving us the same story by saying that Mr Beattie was a bully and a sexual deviant.'

'Is that all?' Messenger asked.

'Well, we can't seem to locate one of the names on the list, and due to the fact that he had a history with Mr Beattie whereas he apparently beat the man, we think it may possibly lead us in the right direction if we were to find him, sir.'

'What was the name?'

'It is, or was, a Jonathon McMullen, sir. But we can't find any records of him whatsoever.'

'Jonathon McMullen you say?'

'Yes, sir,' Taylor replied. He could see the Chief Inspector delve into his memory, trying to place a face to the name.

'Well, just keep me informed Taylor, and keep up the good work. Let's get this over and done with sooner rather than later, yeah?'

'Yes sir, anything we find I will bring to you immediately.'

Messenger headed towards the door and out of his office. Taylor had no intention of sharing any information with the Chief Inspector, as he strongly suspected that the man he looked up to and admired, the person responsible for giving him the chance to run this department ahead of all the qualified local detectives, was heavily involved in this systematic abuse of children throughout the Cumbrian area for the past three decades. Taylor was now not only desperate to expose these people, but he was now hell-bent on bringing everyone involved to justice — including Chief Inspector Messenger. He was now more determined than ever to track down Jonathon McMullen!

Chapter 16

Charles had decided that the time had now come to pay Brian a visit. It had been two weeks since Jim's funeral, and in Charles' eyes the search had quietened down enough for him to operate in the area without raising suspicion and he thought the time had now come for Brian to meet his fate. Charles' initial reasons for his murderous crime-spree stemmed from the resentment and hatred he felt towards his mother for abandoning him to the traumatic childhood he had to endure, hence he took the three girls. However, he had totally pushed those feelings to one side and was now completely overcome with rage and anger; he was determined to exact revenge on the people who had hurt him, including Brian who simply sat by and did nothing! As darkness fell and Charles locked up the surgery behind him, he rang his wife to tell her that he had been called out to an emergency and to just put his dinner in the microwave as he was unsure what time he would make it home. Rebecca just accepted this as the truth and never gave it a second thought.

***

As Charles made his way from Carlisle to Whitehaven, once again his adrenaline kicked in and his heart worked overtime. He started to plan over and over again in his head how he was going to kill Brian, as he hadn't initially intended to do so, unlike the careful planning he'd put into Jim's death. This just added to his excitement, and he sensed the thrill of the unknown the closer he got.

Charles pulled up a few streets away from where Brian lived and made the remainder of the way on foot with only his rucksack with him; the one that he had previously used when he'd visited Haywood farm. He thought about sneaking around the back of the semi-detached house and trying to force his way inside but stopped and thought again. Brian hadn't seen him in twenty-six years; Charles doubted he would be recognised. He decided instead to just knock on the door and take it from there.

Charles then brazenly walked up to the front door of Brian's house and rang the bell. He could see through the window that somebody was home as the TV and lights were on, he casually placed his hand into his jacket pocket and fingered the chloroform-soaked handkerchief as he awaited an answer. Charles gathered his nerve, as he could clearly make out a figure approaching through the stained-glass window.

'Hello,' Brian said, as he set eyes on the unfamiliar man standing in front of him. 'Can I help you?'

Charles' mind went blank. He wanted to just kill the man where he stood, but knew it was too risky and needed to gain entry so he had to think on his feet. Quick as a flash he responded.

'Hi, sorry to bother you at this hour, I was just wondering if ... if ...'

Oh, fuck it. He delivered a swift and precise left hook which connected with Brian's jaw, instantly knocking him off his feet, leaving him unconscious. Charles looked all around him to make sure nobody had witnessed the punch and, happy in the knowledge they hadn't, he swiftly entered the house and closed the door behind him.

As Brian awoke and regained his senses he noticed straight away that his limbs were restricted and his mouth was taped shut. He looked down from his seat where he had been positioned, and panicked as he spied the cable ties that bound his hands and feet. What the fuck was happening? A man sat near him, staring intently at him. After a few moments the strange man spoke.

'Give me one good reason why I should let you live?'

If he wasn't in one hundred percent panic mode before, he certainly was now as he could sense his impending doom. Charles let him dwell on the question and pulled his chair closer to where Brian was sat to let him get a better look at his face. Charles then sniggered as he saw a stream of urine make a trail from Brian's groin, all the way down his beige pants trouser leg to his feet.

'What's the matter, Brian, scared are we? Not a nice feeling is it, being scared and alone and with no one to come to your aid?' Charles was starting to get a real buzz out of humiliating Brian by this point and spoke to him again. 'Let me fill in the gaps for you, Brian. The last time you saw me was in 1989. It was also the year I left the Beatties' farm. The farm in which you placed me, you know the one I am talking about don't you, Brian? The one you used to go and sit in and drink with your good friend Jim!'

Brian knew in that moment exactly who he was now faced with, and knew after the death of Jim that this was not going to end well for him. He just hung his head in shame, as he knew nothing he could say would take away the traumas Jonathon had had to endure.

'What was it you said to Jim all those years ago, Brian? Correct me if I am wrong, but wasn't it, "THAT BOY NEEDS A FIRM HAND", or something to that effect?'

Brian knew, of course, he was referring to the time Jonathon had told him about the incident where Jim had struck Edna and totally dismissed him.

'Well how do you like my firm hand? Not very

pleasant is it?' Charles smiled maliciously. 'Back to what I said before, Brian. Give me one good reason why I should let you live, and maybe I just might.'

Brian knew full well that Jonathon, or whatever his name was these days, had no intention of letting him live, as he wouldn't even remove the tape from his mouth to let him respond. He just took one last look at Charles and hoped in that moment that he would maybe make it fast and painless before hanging his head yet again and awaiting his punishment. He was to get his wish as Charles spoke and said, 'See, just as I thought', then removed the Stanley knife from his bag, approached where Brian was sat and grabbed him by his hair, lifting his head and forcing him to face him before looking into his eyes and dragging the blade across his neck slowly, totally severing his jugular in doing so. Charles held his head aloft for a few seconds and watched as Brian began to bleed out and choke on his own blood before finally letting go and allowing Brian's head to fall to his chest. Charles cleaned the blade by running it down the side of Brian's trouser leg, and again smirked at his urine-stained clothes and realised how pathetic and helpless the old man was in his final moments. Charles just had one last thing to do before leaving the house and once again removed the spray paint from his bag and proceeded to write:

AND GOD SAW THAT THE WICKEDNESS OF MAN WAS GREAT IN THE EARTH, AND THAT EVERY IMAGINATION OF THE THOUGHTS OF HIS HEART WAS ONLY EVIL CONTINUALLY. AND IT REPENTED THE LORD THAT HE HAD MADE MAN ON THE EARTH, AND IT GRIEVED HIM AT HIS HEART. AND THE LORD SAID, I WILL DESTROY MAN WHOM I HAVE CREATED FROM THE FACE OF THE EARTH; BOTH MAN, AND BEAST, AND THE CREEPING THING, AND THE FOWLS OF THE AIR; FOR IT REPENTETH ME THAT I HAVE

*MADE THEM. BUT NOAH FOUND GRACE IN THE
EYES OF THE LORD.*

Charles covered an entire wall in doing so, and
was pleased as he surveyed his work once more
before making his way out of the house unnoticed
and back to where his car was parked.

***

The next morning Taylor informed Georgie that they
would be taking a drive to Whitehaven to once again
speak with Brian Jenkins, although he didn't disclose
to her at this point his recent findings and suspicions.
It wasn't until he got her away from the station and
they were well on their way towards Brian's home
that he pulled the car over and asked her to get out,
just on the off chance that the vehicle may have
been bugged by Chief Inspector Messenger; he'd
decided to entrust and confide in Georgie all about
his discoveries.

'All of what I'm about to tell you is private and
strictly confidential. It stays between us. I have been
monitoring Brian Jenkins' calls and internet activity,
and it seems as though the Chief Inspector, Ian
Messenger, was secretly a member of the paedophile
ring.'

Georgie gasped, but Taylor continued.

'This would explain why none of the victims
came forward, as there were high-ranking figures
of authority involved to dissuade them. We've found
out that victims have recently mentioned the police
being involved in cover-ups, which also makes
sense if Messenger is a suspect. Now, I trust you and
your opinion and would very much like your help in
building a case — off the record, of course — against
the paedophile ring.'

Georgie pondered his request as they walked
slowly back to the car. She knew the pair of them

could potentially be about to commit career suicide if they were to be discovered and then discredited. But, apart from his indiscretions towards his wife, deep down he was a moral man and genuinely wanted to put an end to the corruption and abuse that had plagued the victims' youth.

'Okay, you're on.'

'Thank you. I couldn't do this without you.'

They re-entered the parked car.

'Once we've visited Brian,' Taylor said, 'we can go back to speak with all the victims and bring photographs. See if that jogs the victims' memories; maybe they would be willing to come forward and testify in court.'

Georgie once again admired her partner and respected his decency and professionalism.

***

As they pulled up outside of Brian's home, Taylor immediately sensed something was amiss. It was a bright, spring morning, yet the curtains were still drawn in the front room, and two full milk bottles still sat on the doorstep. He thought it possible that Brian was maybe having a lie in. No, Brian didn't strike him as the kind of man that would lay in his bed till near lunch time... Taylor started thinking he may have committed suicide as he thought the net was closing in on him. At this point Taylor was just speculating but after ringing the bell, then knocking on the door without reply, he looked closer through the stained glass window and could make out a glimmer of light that flickered through what looked like an opening to another room, which convinced him that the TV was still on in the house.

Taylor at this point decided to attempt the door handle and was surprised to find it unlocked. He looked at Georgie in a manner that told her that he thought something wasn't quite right, before calling down the corridor from the doorstep.

'Mr Jenkins, Mr Jenkins, it's Detective Taylor and Georgina Riley, may we come in?'

He could clearly tell by this point that the TV was definitely on, as he heard advert jingles coming from the room, but still did not hear a reply from Brian.

'Stay here!' Taylor whispered to Georgie. His intuition was telling him that something was definitely not right, and he was barely wrong when it came to his gut instincts. The hairs on the back of his neck stood to attention as he cautiously made his way down the hall towards the room where the noise of the TV was coming from.

With the fear of the unknown and thoughts racing through his mind at what he was about to discover, he nervously kicked open the door that led to where Brian's blood soaked body was slumped over on the floor after falling off his chair post mortem.

Taylor could barely look at the magnitude of blood that surrounded the body, and had to cover his mouth and nose with his hand to prevent him from being sick as the stench filled his nostrils.

'You might want to come and take a look at this, but I shall warn you, it's not a pretty sight!' he called back to Georgie.

The first thing she noticed as she entered the room was not the body, but once again the biblical verse upon the wall, confirming that this was once again the work of the same person they were searching for, and also cemented her suspicions of him striking again and again.

Taylor called his findings in to the station, and the two of them inspected the house for any signs of clues until the forensic team attended. Taylor instructed the officers that arrived first on the scene to knock on all of the surrounding houses to see if anybody witnessed anything, but he suspected due to the caution shown in the other cases that once again nothing would arise. He then instructed Georgie to once again follow him to his car.

'It looks as though we need to go back and speak to Minister Davies yet again,' he commented. 'And we also need to speed up our other investigation before the killer gets to everybody else before we can bring them to justice!'

'Look on the bright side, Taylor.'

'What bright side?' he asked.

'Well, at least we have a number of names that he could be possibly targeting next. That at least gives us a bit of an upper hand. If he was to go after them next, we could monitor those people and see if anything suspicious happens.'

'Excellent plan, Georgie, I never thought of that. We make a good team, me and you. The only problem is though, how do we get the manpower without making the Chief Inspector aware?'

'I haven't quite thought that far ahead yet, but leave it with me, I'll try and think of something.'

With that, the two of them set off back towards Carlisle to once again go and speak with Minister Davies.

***

'I half-thought I would be seeing you again, Detective Taylor. And you, Miss Riley. It is a pleasure as always. I wondered how long it would take before the man struck again. I am right in assuming it is the same suspect, aren't I, Detective?'

'I am afraid so, Minister. And what made you so sure he would strike again if you don't mind me asking?'

'It was the anger and revenge-driven meaning of the verse that the killer used, and the brutality in the way he exacted his revenge. Can I ask, Detective, did you find anything to suggest that the victim led a secret life like I previously suggested, maybe hiding his sexuality?'

'Interestingly enough, I was just about to get to that. It appears that the victim, Mr Beattie, was part of some kind of paedophile network that took in vulnerable young children in the care of the local authorities, then subjected these youngsters to prolonged periods of abuse. Going off what you told us, we believe that one of those victims could be the one targeting these men now.'

'But what about the girls, Detective? That's the one thing I just don't get. How are they involved in all of this?'

'That is the million dollar question, Minister. We just don't know either.'

'Back to the matter at hand, then. What can I help you two with this time?'

Georgie spoke next and proceeded to tell Minister Davies all about this morning's gruesome discovery, and repeated the verse that was found on Brian's wall.

'Ah, Genesis 6:5-8. Now this is starting to become clear,' the minister said to a puzzled Taylor and Miss Riley. 'Can I ask you both, how was this victim connected to Mr Beattie?'

'He was the Social worker who referred the majority of the children that passed through the Beattie household throughout this period,' Taylor informed him.

'And do you two believe this man was part of the abuse that took place?' he again questioned.

'We believe at this moment in time that he had some involvement in it. If not the physical act, then he was still most definitely the orchestrator of these children being put into that position, and he was guilty of idly sitting back and allowing it to happen.'

'Well let me tell you what my thoughts on the matter are, and see if that helps you both. This murderer associates himself with Noah, and sees his abusers as the wicked men that God will wipe out. I think you're right; if he wasn't involved in the direct abuse, then the killer would probably associate him with the "creeping thing" from the verse.

'Do you have an extensive list of people who might be involved in the abuse? I can guarantee that the killer, who justifies his actions by believing he is doing God's work by "destroying man from the face of the Earth", will most definitely be targeting these people next. I think you're right that it is undeniably a past victim returning to exact his revenge upon his abusers. The sooner you find your man, the better; his rage and reasoning for his actions are without doubt taking control of his every thought, and he is being driven by carrying out the work of God in his own mind.'

***

Over the next couple of days Taylor and Georgie re-visited all of the people with whom they had previously spoken to regarding their time with the Beatties. As planned, this time they were armed with pictures of all the individuals on the list of people that Brian had contacted in the week leading up to his death. Nearly each and every one of them identified the majority of the men as being their abusers, and over half of them confirmed Taylor's suspicions about Chief Inspector Messenger being involved. They repeatedly pointed him out as being one of the more forceful ones and quite a few of them all stated the same thing, which was that he used to tell them that it was pointless going to the police with any allegations, as he *was* the police and nobody would believe them and they would find themselves in a world of trouble as a result of making up lies.

However, hardly any of them were willing to testify against these men as they were all well-respected pillars of the community, and they thought nobody would believe them due to the amount of time that had passed. Furthermore, they didn't want their pasts to be dragged through the media; they resented having to re-live the awful memories already.

Only one victim agreed to testify in front of a courtroom, on one condition: she wanted to be placed in protective custody until the trial was over. She had lived her whole life in fear of her abusers one day coming back for her, and decided she did not want to live in fear any longer. Taylor agreed to her requests, but knew realistically he could not offer her that at this moment in time as that would involve informing Chief Inspector Messenger of his findings. He decided to pull Georgie to one side and asked her to do him a huge favour for the sake of the case and have the witness stay at the hotel with her; nobody at the station would suspect that. She could stay with Georgie at least until they could gather enough evidence from her about the details of the abuse so he could present a solid case to the Crown Prosecution Service (CPS) against Messenger and the others. They would try to bring the paedophile network to its knees from the top down!

This didn't sit well with Georgie, who already suspected that she was in over her head, but she trusted Taylor, and reluctantly agreed to his request. They gathered the woman's belongings and returned to the hotel where Georgie was staying and informed the woman that she would not be able to leave until she received instructions that it was safe to do so.

***

Taylor went to work by himself the next day as Georgie decided to take the day off and find out as much information as she could from the woman. He made up an excuse on her behalf to the Chief Inspector and told him that he had a couple of leads to follow up on regarding the death of Brian Jenkins. Messenger was by this point starting to become extremely impatient with Taylor and threatened to replace him as lead detective on the case as he suggested that he wasn't up to the job. Taylor did his best to reassure him that he was, and convinced Messenger to give him another few weeks to try and locate the missing Jonathon McMullen, as they had managed to rule out all the other names on the list they had received of all the children that ever stayed with the Beatties.

Taylor addressed his team and asked if there had been any recent developments on the case and, more importantly, in the search for Jonathon McMullen. Everybody was baffled; there were just no leads on his existence, let alone whereabouts turning up. Taylor knew that he was running out of time before the killer struck again, it could be weeks or even days. If only they knew who his next target was going to be, then he might just be able to catch him in the act by having around the clock surveillance on the intended victim. But once again he knew that he could not put that suggestion forward. He just knew that it was probably going to be someone on his list!

As a frustrated Taylor made his way into his office he received a phone call from one of the forensic experts involved in all of the recent deaths.

'Detective Taylor?' the voice on the end of the phone asked.

'Yes? Can I help you?'

'Maybe quite the opposite, Detective. I'm thinking I might be able to help you.'

'How so?' Taylor asked.

'Well, Detective, my name is Frank Sinclair, and I am one of the leading forensic experts that attended at the scene of not only Amber Thompson's body, but the bodies of James Beattie and Brian Jenkins also.'

Taylor's interest was roused. 'Please tell me you've got something good for me?'

'Well, I believe that one of my colleagues has told you already that we picked up a partial foot print on the river bank where Amber's body was discovered?'

'Yes, yes, go on.'

'Well we also managed to get a footprint from

the home of Mr Jenkins due to the amount of blood that was on the floor. And I can now confirm that they are the same size eleven, and exactly identical shoe patterns, which probably confirms that the two murders was committed by the same lone attacker.'

Taylor immediately started to feel deflated at being told something he already knew. 'Is that it?'

'Actually no detective, if you let me finish, I was just about to get to the good part!'

'Which is?' he pressed.

'We also managed to get a partial finger print from the door knob at Haywood farm, which isn't that of Mr Beattie. And that's not all — we also managed to find a hair fibre near to where the body was found that doesn't belong to the victim.'

Taylor thanked the man and told him to get back in touch as soon as the two pieces of evidence had been analysed, and let him know if they manage to present a match. Taylor then immediately left his office and was heading towards Chief Inspector Messenger's to let him know of this recent discovery, but stopped as he approached, deciding against informing his senior. If he was to identify the man responsible he wanted to question him first, before Messenger could take over proceedings and possibly collapse the case Taylor was building against him.

***

It was an anxious wait over the next twenty-four hours as he expected to hear back from Frank Sinclair over the analysis of the evidence, but Taylor was soon elated as he received the phone call stating that they had got a match on the fingerprint, but the hair fibre was unhelpful as it belonged to a bovine animal.

'The match we have on the fingerprint belongs to a Mr Charles Lee. I hope that can help you in your enquiries and you manage to find the sick bastard behind these murders, Detective. In all my years in forensics, I have never witnessed anything like that of the discovery at Haywood farm.'

Taylor agreed and assured Frank that he would keep him updated on any progress it might lead to, before hanging up and going to his team and quietly asking them to get any details on a Mr Charles Lee that lived or worked in the local area, but to keep it between them at this moment in time as it might not be any use at all.

Got you! One of his staff gave him the details on Mr Charles Lee and continued to tell him that he was a local veterinarian in Carlisle and handed him not only the address of his practice, but his home address also.

***

Meanwhile back at the hotel, Georgie was gathering loads of evidence on the people behind the abuse from the cooperating victim. She had dates, times, places and now names of the people involved after carefully studying the photos over and over again. Georgie could not believe that these so-called "respectable" figures in the community operated at the highest levels inside the network. She was just about to call Taylor and inform him of the in depth of the knowledge she had managed to gain when he actually called her.

Before she could tell him what she had discovered, he excitedly blurted out, 'I think we've fucking got him, Georgie!'

'Jonathon McMullen? You mean you've managed to find him?' she asked, totally forgetting everything she was about to tell him.

'Possibly Georgie, except this guy's name is Charles Lee. He's a local veterinarian and knows the area, but also, the forensic team managed to pick up a partial fingerprint from Beattie's door handle and it matched his!'

He then informed her that he needed her to accompany him to go and question Charles Lee immediately, so she would have to leave the woman alone in her hotel room for a few hours. This news didn't go down too well with the witness when Georgie relayed this information to her, but Georgie reassured her that everything would be fine and that she would be back within a couple of hours.

As Georgie made her way down the foyer and out towards the car park, she was so absorbed in her own thoughts and anxieties about the man she was going to interview with Taylor, that she totally failed to notice Chief Inspector Messenger waiting patiently outside. Unbeknownst to Taylor and Georgie, Chief Inspector Messenger had been running his own investigations ever since the death of James Beattie. Just as Taylor had kept records on Brian Jenkins' calls and internet activity, Messenger had been monitoring Taylor's activities and knew exactly what they had been up to. He could not let their evidence become public, and so he'd waited. Finally his opportunity had come; Georgie had left the witness alone and vulnerable. He knew what he had to do.

***

As Taylor and Georgie made their short journey to Charles' practice, Georgie gave him her theory on it all, stating how it all made perfect sense; Mr Lee was a veterinarian, he would have access to Ketamine, which was found at Amber Thompson's post mortem. Also he would have an in depth knowledge of the areas in which the murders had taken place. And when Taylor told her that his home address was situated in the Scottish borders, this confirmed things even more, due to the disappearance of Lucy Mitchell from Gretna. The fact that James Beattie was murdered on his own farm only solidified this theory. There were just two things that did not add up. Why the girls? And what of the main suspect Jonathon McMullen?

Charles instantly recognised the detective and his assistant from the news and papers as he caught a glimpse of them from his office window getting out of their car and making their way towards the practice. Sheer panic and a sense of impending dread took control of him as he sat and waited for Linda to show them through. He could not understand how they had managed to find him, as he had been so careful to cover his tracks. He thought about making a run for it, but knew this would only add to his guilt. Instead all he could do was straighten himself up and try to play it cool and just see exactly what they knew.

Linda showed the two of them to Charles' office and knocked before entering, explaining to her boss how the two had come to ask him a few questions. Charles looked up from where he sat and politely invited them to make their way inside and take a seat. He then thanked Linda and asked her if she wouldn't mind preparing some coffee for the visitors, immediately putting on the charm offensive, all the while secretly scared to death about what would happen next.

As Linda made her way out of his office, Taylor thanked Charles for the offer of coffee and also for taking the time to speak with them and try and help them with their enquiries. The first thing Georgie noticed was the scar that ran along Charles' jaw line and she discreetly made Taylor aware of it also, taking them back to their first meeting and her initial profiling of the suspect.

'So, how may I be of assistance, Detective…?'

'Taylor, it's Taylor.'

'Yes, right, Detective Taylor.'

'Yes, and this is my partner, Detective Riley.'

Charles instantly picked up on this lie, as he knew exactly who she was, and knew that she wasn't a detective, but chose to go along with the lie to avoid suspicion.

'Like I was saying, how may I be of assistance to you?'

'We were wondering how well you knew one of the recent victims in a murder case we are currently investigating. Mr James Beattie, to be more precise?'

'Ah yes, Mr Beattie, I heard of his tragic death on the local news. I hope you can find the person responsible, Detectives.'

'We're working on it, Mr Lee, I can assure you of that. So did you know the victim at all then, Charles? You don't mind if I call you Charles do you?'

'Not at all, Detective Taylor. I prefer it, it makes things a lot less formal.' Charles did not know how else to respond as he couldn't be sure how much they knew at this point, if anything at all.

Taylor, sensing his hesitance then added, 'The thing is, Mr Lee, our team of forensic experts have discovered a fingerprint which belongs to you at the scene of the crime, and we are just looking to find out if there was a reason for this?'

Charles' hands were clammy at this point. What excuse could he offer as to his print being found? How could this have happened? He'd specifically remembered to put on his surgical gloves before entering. Then all of a sudden he remembered being at the farm a few months before, which immediately started to calm his nerves as he knew this would give him an explanation. He knew he had a record of the visit and a copy of the invoice he sent to Jim to back this up. His nerves instantly started to settle, and he composed himself before explaining to the pair how he had visited Mr Beattie's farm a few months earlier to tend to one of his cows, and that Mr Beattie had invited him inside of his home and made him coffee and thanked him for his work. He further added that he had not seen the man before that day, or had any further contact with him since. He then confidently pulled out a copy of his records from his filing cabinet, confirming what he had just told them. He went on to state that Mr Beattie was a very welcoming, friendly old man that did not strike him as the kind of man who would have any enemies that would want him dead. Taylor's elation soon dissipated as what he was told made perfect sense, and with no other concrete evidence to put forward against Charles, he accepted that they had the wrong man at this point and thanked Charles for his time and explained that they may need to speak to him again at some point, but as for now that was all.

'Just one more thing, Detective...' Charles said, as his inquisitive narcissistic mind took over as they made their way towards the door.

'What's that, Charles?' Taylor replied.

'It just occurred to me, you said that you discovered a fingerprint that matched mine at the scene. How is this even possible given the fact that I have never been in trouble with the police or broken a law to my knowledge in my entire life?'

'I believe you are an ex-military man, Charles, is that correct?'

'Yes, that is correct, Detective. What does that have anything to do with this?' Charles asked, confused as to where this was leading.

'I also believe you spent a bit of time in the Glass House before you left?' Taylor asked him, letting him know in doing so that he had done his homework on him.

'Ah, now I get it.' The penny had finally dropped: his time in military prison had caught up with him.

'Yes Charles, even our minor discrepancies of our youth come back to haunt us at some point.'

Charles could only offer a faint laugh as he replied, 'Indeed they do, Detective, indeed they do.'

How could he have forgotten that? He mentally kicked himself for being so unusually careless as they left the practice.

***

Taylor's frustrations were running high as he gave Georgie a lift back to the station, and he became snappy towards her for no other reason than this frustration.

'That was another fucking waste of time, and we're still no closer to finding Jonathon McMullen! Please tell me you managed to get something good from our witness for God's sake?'

'I did, but I'll get back to that. In the meantime — and I don't mean to be rude — but are you totally overlooking the obvious, Taylor?'

'What do you mean?'

'Did you not see the way in which Charles squirmed when you mentioned the fingerprint at Beattie's farm? Or his scar? Also, did you not see the way he looked at us? I got the impression he knew exactly who we are, yet chose not to question you when you introduced me as Detective Riley.'

'We can't go off your gut feeling though can we, Georgie!' Taylor said, frustrated. 'The fact is, that Charles has a valid reason for being at the farm, and there is absolutely no motive at this point that we know of to suggest otherwise.'

This suddenly stirred something in Georgie. 'You know you said that Mr Lee was previously in the military, which suggests you researched his past?'

'Yeah, well obviously! And?'

'Did you look into his childhood also? And did you speak to anybody in his regiment that might shed some light on his character and why he left?'

Taylor sensed she was onto something as he realised he never had any details on Charles before joining the army...very strange.

Taylor and Georgie then went back to the station to ask his team to run a full background check on Mr Charles Lee, and told them to get back on the phone to the people at the deed poll office and see if they could offer anything else on either Jonathon McMullen or Charles Lee. He then told Georgie that he would come back to the hotel with her and get a full written and recorded statement from their witness to have ready to hand into the CPS as soon as the time comes.

***

On the opposite side of the city to where Taylor and Georgie had been questioning Charles, Chief Inspector Messenger had got out of his own personal car and, in plain clothes and pulling on a baseball cap in an effort to disguise his recently high profile face, cautiously approached the entrance of the hotel. He made his way to the second floor bedroom where he had seen Georgie through her window whilst he'd sat anxiously observing from the car park.

'Room service,' he said as he knocked on the door.

The woman was slightly alarmed at this; she certainly hadn't ordered any room service as she didn't want to abuse Georgie's hospitality and trust. A second knock rang out and the woman nervously made her way toward the locked door and took a look through the spy hole. She could make out the figure of a man. He had his back to her so she could not be sure if it was genuinely room service or somebody coming to harm her.

'I'm sorry but you have the wrong room, I didn't order any room service,' she called back in an attempt to get the man to turn and face her.

Messenger was getting angry now; he did not want to be out in the corridor any longer and draw attention to himself so turned and faced the door, not realising she was looking right at him from behind it. As she realised just exactly who it was she let out a slight gasp, which immediately informed Messenger that she knew who he was and his reason for being there. With that in mind, and not wanting to give her the time to call for help, he looked both ways to see that nobody was looking, and with one swift kick he booted open the door, which smacked back into the woman's face.

He immediately recognised her as one of his victims as he made his way inside, closing the door behind him. She desperately tried to scramble to her feet as he approached her, taking out a length of rope from his pocket as he neared.

'Please, stop!' she begged, as he silently and purposefully positioned the rope around her neck, then proceeded to pull the ends tightly around her throat, cutting off her air supply in doing so.

He watched as her face reddened and she started to lose consciousness due to her lack of oxygen, and held his stance until she had totally given into it and her body went limp. In that instance he heard voices coming from the corridor; he let the rope slacken and removed it completely, placing it back in his pocket. He then went and looked through the spy hole. Fortunately for him it was just a passing couple making their way back to their room, and as soon as they closed their door behind them, he opened the door to the room he was in and made his way into the corridor, closing the door behind him again, safe in the knowledge that she would never be able to speak out against his crimes ever again.

Chapter 17

As Taylor and Georgie made their way towards the hotel, Taylor instantly spotted Messenger's Audi as it teared away down the road that led into the carpark entrance, heading in the opposite direction of where they were going. Taylor knew straight away that the woman had possibly been harmed or even killed, and immediately informed Georgie to call an ambulance on the off chance that she might still be alive. He also knew in that moment that Messenger was fully aware of what he and Georgie were trying to accomplish and would without doubt try and do everything in his power to stop himself from being exposed, but also do his utmost to discredit not only Taylor, but Georgie also.

Everything depended on what state they found the witness in, and the two of them ran inside the hotel, pushing past everyone in their way as they did so, in a desperate attempt to try and help the woman. As they nervously opened the door they both looked at each other and thought they were too late, as they was greeted by the sight of her laying on the floor in only a dressing gown to cover her modesty, totally unconscious and foaming at the mouth.

Georgie immediately sprang into action as Taylor got back on the phone to check how long the ambulance would be. Georgie felt enormous guilt, as she felt responsible for being a part of the circumstances that enabled this to happen.

She looked up at Taylor. 'It doesn't look good, I can't find a pulse!' She was determined to try and keep the woman alive though, and started to administer CPR until the paramedics attended on scene a few minutes later.

Taylor just stood there, feet firmly rooted to the floor as he watched and hoped and prayed that she would pull through — not just for her sake, but so he could bring the bastard, Messenger, to his knees!

The attending paramedics tried relentlessly to resuscitate the woman for what seemed like an eternity as the pair of Taylor and Riley looked on in sheer hope that she would make it. The lead paramedic had given up as his efforts to resuscitate had all failed, and was just about to pronounce the woman dead, when all of a sudden her foot involuntarily moved, forcing him to re-check to see if she was breathing. He could not believe it as he found the slightest trace of a pulse and shouted at his colleague to get the stretcher as he put an oxygen mask over her face.

Georgie insisted she would stay with the woman on the way to the hospital and until she regained consciousness, if at all, to avoid any further harm coming to her. Taylor, as in any other case, called for forensics and another team of detectives to come and gather evidence.

***

After Taylor handed over the crime scene to his colleagues from CID, he decided to make his way back to the station to face Messenger, knowing full well that he was now probably going to be taken off the case.

'Still nothing on Jonathon McMullen, sir,' came a voice from one of his junior staff as he made his way towards the Chief Inspector's office.

Messenger beckoned him in through the window and Taylor entered the office and slammed the door shut behind him. Messenger immediately started to question his detective on what he had been told from all the names they had interviewed regarding their time at the Beatties'.

'I know everything, *sir*!' he angrily snapped back at Messenger, desperately resisting the urge to beat his boss to a bloody pulp and arrest him in front of all the other officers. However, he knew at this point that without the witness' statement, he had nothing concrete on Messenger and he would probably walk free if correct procedures didn't take place.

'Well you tell me what you think you know, and I will tell you what I know,' Messenger provokingly asked Taylor.

'I know that you are a fucking disgusting piece of shit, that has raped and tortured innocent children for the past twenty-five years, and have totally abused your position of trust! I also know that, you and your so-called "respectable" friends have run a secret paedophile ring for all this time, and it is just a matter of time before I expose you all for what you are!'

'Is that so, Detective?' Messenger replied smugly. 'Now let me tell you what I know, shall I? He reached into his desk, removed a large envelope and passed it to Taylor to look at.

'What is this?' Taylor asked nervously.

'Why don't you take a look inside and find out for yourself?'

Taylor hesitantly opened the package and removed its contents. He was shocked to see semi-naked pictures of himself and Georgie from the night he spent in her hotel room. He realised somebody had obviously crept in as they slept and taken the pictures without them knowing.

This case was far too big to just let go of, but on the other hand it would break his wife's heart to once again discover he had been unfaithful. Also, he didn't want Georgie's career destroyed over one drunken mistake. Taylor found himself in a dilemma as he contemplated which way to play his next move.

'What do you think your wife would think if she was

to wake up to these through her letterbox tomorrow morning, Taylor?' Messenger sneered. 'Better yet, what do you think the papers will make of them when they realise that instead of tracking down a killer, you and Miss Riley have been drunkenly cavorting in hotel rooms like teenagers?'

Taylor was extremely annoyed at himself now; he knew he should have conducted himself more professionally, and knew that Georgie would not want naked pictures of herself that could possibly destroy her career in the national news.

'You see, Detective, you're not the only smart one around here. You might have been investigating me, but I was also following your every move and everything you spoke of on the phone... Just one last thing before you leave, Detective Taylor.'

'Which is?' Taylor replied, defeated.

'If you thought for one second that that stupid woman was going to bring me down, then you were sadly mistaken. It's just a shame that she will never be able to give you any more information now, isn't it?'

'Actually, *sir*, there is a good chance that she may pull through, and I hope and pray that she does so I can bring you down!'

'Needless to say, Taylor, you are now officially off the case. As of now you are on permanent vacation — that's not a request, it is an order. Now get the fuck out of my sight!' Messenger tried to play it cool, but deep down he was raging with himself for not finishing the woman off properly and putting an end to all of this.

***

As Taylor cleared his desk, one of the officers from his team came in to see him and update him on the progress of the hunt for the killer.

'Sir, after speaking with the guys at the deed poll office, they have confirmed that Charles Lee was definitely known by another name at some point as they have details on his name transfer. Unfortunately though, they seem to have misplaced all the documentation of what his previous name was. They have told me that they will try their best to locate it over the next few days and will contact us as soon as they find anything.'

'Good work, Detective,' Taylor replied. He explained that Messenger had just taken him off the case, and proceeded to tell him that although he wouldn't be in the office, he would still be continuing with his investigations into the case from the outside, and instructed his junior that if him and the others find out any more information they should contact him directly and not give this information to Messenger. He couldn't let him know the reasons why, but just asked the man to trust his judgement, as he had done so many times in the past, to great success.

'You got it, Boss.' The junior detective knew that Taylor was a brilliant detective and a good boss, and knew he must have good reasons for his actions.

Meanwhile at Carlisle's Cumberland Infirmary, a guilt-ridden Georgina Riley sat attentively outside the room of the witness, tirelessly waiting for any signs of her pulling through. This was their doing, hers and Taylor's. They both had blood on their hands if this woman didn't make it. What a tragic shame it would be if she passed away at the hands of one of the people that subjected her to a catalogue of abuse as a child, someone who subjected her to a lifetime of fear. Georgie seriously contemplated walking away from Taylor and the case, but stopped herself; she knew she would never be able to live with herself and conscience if she didn't help Detective Taylor get justice for the victims and rid Cumbria of these vile predators.

It was at this point that Taylor called Georgie and informed her that Messenger had taken him off the case. That meant she was, too. He then nervously explained to her about the pictures he had just seen from their night in her hotel room. Georgie didn't know how to respond, and Taylor could tell by the silence on the end of the line that she was completely in shock, and told her he was on his way over to the hospital to see her.

When he arrived, he immediately made his way down the corridor towards where Georgie was seated with her head in her hands. He could clearly make out that she had been crying and he instantly sat next to her and put his arm around her in a comforting manner. It was at this point that Georgie threw her arms around him and clung tight as she broke down in his arms and realised she was in way over her head and admitted to Taylor that she was scared, scared that some of these powerful men might be intending to come after her next and told him that she did not feel safe. Taylor tried his best to reassure her that he would keep her safe, but she knew that even he could not protect her if they were to target her next.

Taylor couldn't think of anything else to say other than, 'Come and stay at my house, just until this is all over.' He knew it was far too unsafe for her to return to her hotel room. Just look at what had happened to the witness!

'Thanks, Taylor. It's a kind offer and I know you mean well, but I just couldn't look your wife in the eyes knowing what we did.'

He knew she was right; he had not thought that far ahead.

'So what are you going to do?'

'Well, I am not leaving this hospital until she wakes up, that's for sure. I can't bear the thought of leaving her vulnerable and alone twice, knowing that we put her in this position when she was trying to help us!'

'And what have the doctors said?'

'They're still not sure if she will pull through, as they can't be certain how long it was before she was resuscitated. They've also said that, because they can't be sure how long her brain was starved of oxygen, they don't know if she will be in a vegetative state if she was to wake up.'

Taylor so badly wanted to believe that she would wake and give him the statement he desperately needed. Knowing that Messenger knew that she was still alive, albeit not in any fit state to talk, he thought it a good idea that Georgie stayed, just in case Messenger or somebody else came back to try and finish her off. He then offered to go back to her hotel room to gather the rest of her belongings, as she hadn't had chance to do so since leaving there in the ambulance.

'I'll go and grab your stuff from the hotel, Georgie. I know we're officially off the case, but I still fully intend on bringing this to a conclusion and getting justice for the witness and the murdered victims against Messenger and the murderer. My team remain loyal to me. We *will* solve this, Georgie. I reckon you were right about Charles Lee — my colleague found out that he had changed his name via deed poll years ago. We are waiting to hear back from them any day now as to whether he used to be called Jonathon McMullen.'

'Please just be careful, Taylor. I don't want to be having to sit beside two hospital beds over the next few days, or worse still!'

Taylor could sense the sincerity and care towards him from her. In a non-sexual way, he gently placed a kiss on her forehead and assured her that he would be fine, before leaving her to watch over the witness whilst he went and collected her belongings.

Chapter 18

Charles failed to tell Rebecca that he had been visited by the police, as he knew it would lead to a whole new line of questioning and suspicion from his wife and couldn't bear the thought of her actually thinking he was capable of doing such things. He instead chose to remain quiet and try and figure out a way of throwing the police off his scent. He could sense that the net was closing in on him though, and if he could not get to all his intended targets before the police got to him, then there was just one last thing he needed to do, which was to find and kill Chief Inspector Messenger. At least he would be easy to locate as opposed to his other abusers. He had been so high-profile as of late; it wouldn't be hard to track him down and hand him his fate.

He never expected the opportunity to present itself so quickly though, as he discovered after watching the news the very next day; Chief Inspector Messenger had decided to once again address the media. He explained how they had a very strong suspicion that they knew who the suspect was in connection to all the recent abductions and murders in the area over the past six months, and then pleaded with anybody who knows or knew of a Jonathon McMullen to please come forward and help them with their investigation. Charles knew that it was only a matter of time before he was discovered, and set about developing a plan to find and kill the Chief Inspector before he got to him.

***

The Chief Inspector, not knowing that Taylor's team had discovered that Charles Lee hadn't always being known by that name, was doing all he could to stop the news of him and his accomplices' wicked crimes being exposed. He rashly decided to send out that plea in an effort to try and find Jonathon McMullen and hopefully send out an armed response unit to dispose of him before he had a chance to speak out about his reasons for his actions in recent months. He knew that if that bitch in the hospital didn't wake up, and he managed to find and kill Jonathon, then all that is left is hearsay and unwilling witnesses. He also knew that if Detective Taylor and Georgina Riley tried to expose him, not only did he have the photographic evidence of their night together, he also knew he could destroy them career-wise by exposing the fact that they placed a witness alone in a hotel room, leaving her to be the victim of an attempted murder — or better yet, a murder victim if she never wakes up.

Less than twenty-four hours later, one of the Chief Inspector's staff alerted him that there was a call for him from a woman who wished to remain anonymous, but had observed his plea on the TV and maybe had some information that could help in the search for Jonathon. Messenger sat and listened intently as the woman told him all the details of the night she gave birth to Jonathon, and how she had desperately in vain been trying to contact him over the years, but that the trail went dead by the time her son had turned sixteen. Messenger let the woman continue as she told him Jonathon's date of birth and other details, but he already had all of this information from Brian before his death, and also remembered what Jonathon looked like as a child, so everything the woman told him was irrelevant. What he needed was someone who knew his whereabouts right now, not forty years ago. He politely thanked the anonymous woman and hung up, no further forward than he was to begin with.

***

Unbeknownst to Messenger, as he was trying to trace down the whereabouts of Jonathon, Charles had actually begun to follow him. He had called Linda and told her to once again clear his schedule for the week, as he wasn't feeling up to coming into work, but neglected to tell Rebecca this. He did not want to raise suspicion and wanted to keep up appearances at home, thus giving him the opportunity to be out all day planning how he was going to ensnare the Chief Inspector.

After following Messenger home from the station that evening, Charles watched as the Chief Inspector left his family home in Brampton, just nine miles from Carlisle, at eight o'clock the following morning, and once again followed him to the station, arriving at twenty minutes past the hour. He did this for the following few days to try and build a picture of his routines. Who he spoke to, the places he visited, what time he took a lunch break...anything to help him get a better understanding and clearer idea of how and when to strike without being seen.

Taylor was also cautiously tailing Messenger and Charles, driving around in an unmarked hire car he had recently leased in an effort to remain inconspicuous and out of sight of the team of detectives Messenger had obviously placed on him.

Taylor had a rough idea of what Charles was planning, but chose to sit on this information and see how it unfolded. He knew if he was to catch Charles in the act before it was too late, it would pave his way back into the force, and he secretly hoped that Charles would then help him expose Messenger and his network, although he knew that this was a long shot.

***

Three days had passed since Taylor's witness had been admitted into Carlisle's Cumberland Infirmary with Georgie by her side, and the chances of her making a full recovery were dwindling. Taylor was seriously starting to despair; he knew it was just a matter of time before Charles was to strike again. Although he hoped Charles would help him bring down Messenger and the paedophile network, he couldn't be sure, and was praying for his witness to wake. He also hoped that he seriously hadn't made an error in judgement by putting all his eggs in one basket in believing that Charles was definitely Jonathon, the man they were looking for.

His suspicions were confirmed the very next day when he received a call from his staff member, the one he had asked not to speak to Messenger if he found any further developments into the search for Jonathon McMullen.

'Hello, sir,' came a quiet voice down the end of line as Taylor answered his mobile. 'I can't really say much right now, sir, as Messenger and his team of detectives are scrutinising every bit of evidence that you and Miss Riley uncovered, and are wanting to know everything about the case. What I can say though, sir, is that you were right about Charles Lee being Jonathon McMullen; I've just got off the phone to deed poll and they have eventually located the records and confirmed your suspicions. The only problem is, sir, I don't know how long I can sit on this information before I will have to inform Messenger of my findings.'

Taylor was overjoyed at hearing this news, and thanked his junior for coming to him first, and also complimented him on his good work before asking, 'Who else knows about what you've just told me?'

'Nobody, sir, like I said, I've just this minute got off

the phone, and I immediately called you.'

'Right, this means I need to act fast. I just need you to give me at least forty-eight hours before you reveal this information to Messenger, and he sends out an armed response unit to bring him in or —' Taylor stopped himself from finishing his sentence, as he knew if he was to say take him down, this would cause the man to ask questions.

'Like I said, sir, I don't know how long I can sit on this, but I will try my best to give you the time you need. Just be aware, Messenger has really got his teeth into this now, sir, and he's determined to bring it to a swift end!'

Before Taylor had time to thank the man once more, the voice on the other end said, 'I've got to go, sir, good luck, and I'll be in touch.'

The line went dead.

Taylor, his thoughts racing, immediately contacted Georgie and informed her he was on his way over to the hospital, as what he was about to tell her he couldn't over the phone. Georgie knew he must've unearthed something, and waited with anticipation until he arrived.

'You were right, Georgie, it's him, it's Charles Lee. He was, and is, Jonathon McMullen!' His tone was excited but hushed; he didn't want to alert anybody that might be eavesdropping in on their conversation.

'How do you know?' she asked him.

Taylor then relayed to her everything he had heard over the phone, and continued to tell her that Messenger was determined to track the killer down before he could reach him, and probably kill him and stop the risk of him speaking out against him. Georgie once again implored Taylor to be careful, as she could sense that this case was about to come to a climax and feared for her colleague; she knew that Messenger, being hell bent on ending the case and stopping himself from being exposed, he would do absolutely anything to make that happen. She feared that he would even kill one of his own officers, as he seemed to have had no qualms about trying to kill their witness to save his own skin.

Chapter 19

Rebecca was starting to realise that something wasn't right at home, and started to suspect that Charles was maybe having an affair; he hadn't touched her in weeks and was spending a lot more time away from the house than he had been as of late. Also, he had become so distracted and snappy towards her and the girls, which caused her to believe that something definitely wasn't right. She asked him what it was that he was up to that was making him act so irrational and out of character.

Charles was obviously far past telling her the real reason for his recent mood swings and late nights out of the home. He assured her that he wasn't having an affair, and that he wasn't even remotely interested in being with another woman. He once again blamed the stresses of work, and lied by telling her that one of the other vets from the practice was on long-term sick leave so he was picking up his colleague's work load so that the practice didn't lose money.

It was plausible, she thought. She then reminded him of his promise not that long ago, where he said he would be taking more of a backseat role at work and leaving the others to take care of things. He then reassured her that he had meant every word of it, and told her how everything would be back to normal very soon. In his head, 'very soon' meant 'upon dealing with Messenger,' but obviously omitted this part.

He was totally delusional at this stage; his mind was overcome with thoughts of vengeance. He knew the police had their suspicions and were possibly building a case against him, but he wasn't going to let that stop him. He continued to plot Messenger's death, thinking he'd better do it sooner rather than later in order to lay all of this to rest and get back to a stable family life.

***

The weekend was steadily approaching, and Charles thought to himself that this would be the perfect time to strike; Messenger never worked weekends, preferring instead to leave the station in the hands of his trusted staff. Charles figured that if he could get him away from his house and out of sight of his wife and kids, he could take him away somewhere remote and spend some real "quality time" with him.

He thought about possibly taking him to the makeshift dungeon that Lucy Mitchell and Sarah Davidson were buried in, but suddenly remembered how bad the stench of rotting flesh had been the last time he had been there. Then it came to him — why not re-visit Haywood farm? There wouldn't be any activity there now as it had been a few weeks since Beattie's death. What's more, it would be a fitting place to kill the Chief Inspector, as it was whilst staying with the Beatties that young Charles had been introduced to Messenger when he was a young, abusive junior police officer.

Once again, Charles carefully and purposefully prepared his rucksack with all the instruments he had used in the past, only this time he added a blow torch and a pair of pliers, as he wasn't going to let him get off relatively lightly as he had Brian. No, this time he was going to spend a full weekend slowly torturing Messenger in the worst ways he could possibly imagine.

He then informed Rebecca how he would be attending another conference for the weekend, and tried to convince her that he had mentioned it a few months earlier, but she knew he was lying and had said no such thing. All she could do was trust her husband's words, but she would also be looking for any tell-tale signs of an affair upon his return. She strongly suspected that the other woman was possibly Linda, Charles' receptionist from work.

***

Taylor had been cautiously following Charles, who was following Messenger over the past few days, and knew his time was running out before the details of Charles being Jonathon were released. In a way, he secretly hoped that Charles would go after the Chief Inspector anytime now so he could maybe catch him in the act and bring the two of them to justice, putting an end to this nightmare. When he'd taken on the case, he'd never expected just how complex and deep-rooted it would turn out to be — well, who would have?

He sat two hundred yards back from where Messenger lived, on this Friday evening in early May 2014, watching from afar for any signs of Charles exiting his Volvo and approaching the Chief Inspector's home. Taylor was exhausted and looked unkempt and dishevelled; the pressure of the last week had totally taken its toll on him by now. He was somewhat relieved to see Charles start his engine and pass by where he was purposely hidden, heading away from Messenger's home. Taylor knew Charles couldn't be planning on going after him tonight, so he decided he would go home and try and get a few hours' sleep and maybe a hot meal, instead of the stale service station sandwiches and pasties he had been getting by on over the past few days. He also needed a shower; he was starting to stink due to him sitting in the car for hours on end in the warm May sunlight. He headed home.

***

Saturday morning arrived and Taylor's wife knew that her husband didn't have to be in work today, so she let him have a lie in and didn't bother to wake him. She could tell he had been overdoing it recently and thought it would do him good to have a long sleep to recharge his batteries. He was absolutely furious when he woke up at half past nine and rushed downstairs to where his wife was preparing breakfast. When Taylor turned on the news he heard local journalist, Jennifer Metcalfe, address the camera.

'...it seems as though police have made significant steps towards finding the killer behind the series of murders in the local area. Inside sources tell us that officers will be apprehending their suspect over the next twenty-four hours and will address the public again in due course...'

Taylor knew this could only mean one thing: that Messenger had managed to obtain the information on Charles, and it was only a matter of time before he probably killed his suspect.

Taylor berated his wife for letting him oversleep, and informed her that he did actually have to be in work today — he hadn't actually got round to telling her about Messenger not only taking him off the case, but in doing so, ending his time at the station, as he would never be able to return if Messenger was to remain in charge. Taylor threw on his clothes and raced out of the house to his waiting car and immediately sped away and raced to Messenger's home on the off-chance that he might not have left the house yet.

It was too late; there was no sign of Messenger's Audi. Taylor automatically assumed that he must be heading up the armed response team in the search for Charles. As he frantically pondered his next move he was interrupted by his phone ringing. As he rummaged through his pocket and removed his mobile, he saw that it was Georgie calling and answered.

'Taylor, it's good news!' she exclaimed excitedly. 'She's pulled through, she's going to be ok. And better yet, she is still willing to testify against Messenger, as she remembers everything that happened in my hotel room and is now more determined than ever to bring him down. You need to get here ASAP and obtain a statement so you can present a case to the CPS and finish that bastard once and for all!'

Taylor couldn't believe his luck. 'Fantastic! I'll be right there. Georgie...have you seen the news this morning?'

Georgie didn't have a clue at what he was getting at as she hadn't seen the news for days due to her bedside vigil. 'No, why?'

'From what I can gather, they must be aware of Charles being Jonathon, and have said they should have the suspect apprehended and in custody by the end of the day!'

'Do you know where he is?'

'No, I'm afraid I overslept and lost the trail, as when I got to Messenger's he and Charles had already left,' Taylor reluctantly explained.

'You should try to find them' Georgie said earnestly. 'I'll stay here and keep the witness safe until you can get the statement to apprehend Messenger.'

Taylor agreed. 'Y'know, you really are brilliant at what you do, Georgie. It's been an honour working alongside you.'

Georgie, sensing he was getting slightly emotional, possibly due to the very real fact that he may never see her again, jokingly replied, 'Stop with the soppy shit, Taylor, and go and finish our work. Put an end to this!'

With that, he promised her that everything would work out and hung up the phone.

***

Meanwhile, at Carlisle police headquarters, the Chief Inspector's team of detectives, alongside the Armed Tactical Response Unit, waited patiently for Messenger to arrive and command the operation to execute a warrant at Charles Lee's home address. Everybody was wondering what the holdup was. They were starting to become restless and impatient as one of his team had spoken to him just over an hour ago and was told that he would be there immediately, after receiving the information about Charles Lee's change of name, totally ruining his plans of a round of golf this sunny Saturday morning.

He would not be arriving this morning, though. Nobody knew that Charles had orchestrated a plan; as Messenger had made his way to the station, Charles had 'accidentally' run into the back of Messenger's Audi on a quiet stretch of country road. As the Chief Inspector had approached him to exchange details, Charles had once again subdued his victim as he grabbed him roughly around the neck and quickly anaesthetised Messenger with his trusty chloroform before lifting him into the boot of his Volvo. He then casually parked up Messenger's Audi by the side of the road and turned off the engine before walking back to his own car and driving away with the unconscious Messenger in the boot.

Chapter 20

Another hour had passed at the station and the detectives weren't prepared to wait any longer for Messenger to arrive; they decided to execute the warrant on Charles' home address without him.

Taylor was parked up outside of the station and positioned in a manner which allowed him to view the Armed Tactical Response Unit preparing to leave the car park alongside other detectives from the department, but they could not see him. He thought it very strange that there was no sign of Messenger, though. After thoroughly scanning the car park he thought it even stranger that there wasn't even any sign of his Audi. Taylor knew something didn't add up, and in that instance he knew that Charles, as he had been all along, was once again one step ahead of the people at Carlisle constabulary, and had managed to abduct Messenger that morning. Taylor once again kicked himself for not getting up sooner! He did not know which way to turn now, and once again got on the phone to Georgie. He begged her for answers as to where he could possibly be taking him. He knew he wouldn't have much time, as Charles generally killed his victims within hours of taking them. Georgie, too, was at a loss, and at that moment in time did not have any answers or even suggestions of where he might have taken him.

***

Charles had managed to avoid detection and, pulling

off the main road, he headed up the dirt track that led to Haywood farm, luckily managing to remain unseen from any neighbouring farmers. He pulled his Volvo into the open barn at the rear of the building, thus hiding it from sight or alerting anybody to any activity at the farm. Charles removed the police tape from across the back door and hopefully checked to see if the door was unlocked. Realising that it wasn't, he then made his way to the rear window that looked into the dining room where he had sat and drank coffee with Jim. After taking a look all around to make sure nobody could see or hear him, he picked up a stone and smashed out a section of glass in the corner of the frame and placed his hand inside and opened the window — all the while Messenger remained blissfully unaware of what Charles had planned as he remained unconscious in the boot.

Charles then climbed inside the building and managed to unlock the back door using the key that hung on the wall beside it, before making his way back over to the Volvo, opening the boot, then placing cable ties around Messenger's limbs in the same fashion he had with the other victims. He also took some tape from his rucksack that was positioned on the parcel shelf and taped the man's mouth shut, just in case he was to wake as he was being transported over Charles' shoulder from the vehicle to the farmhouse. Messenger never woke, however, as he was carried over Charles' shoulder. After locking the kitchen door Charles once again returned to the room in which he had previously taken care of Jim and placed Messenger in the same chair in which Jim had been sleeping. He proceeded to tie him to the chair to eliminate the chance of him escaping once he woke, then stood back and marvelled in the words that were still daubed on the wall in black paint. He revelled in the moment, remembering all the reasons behind his actions — past and present.

***

At the Lee household, Rebecca and the girls received the fright of their lives as they watched as the team of police vehicles raced down the long drive that led to their cottage, jumping in terror as the door was taken clean off its hinges with one almighty thump of the tactical battering ram.

Rebecca clung to the girls for dear life as the Armed Tactical Response Unit swamped every room of the house in search of Charles, the red-lasered spots from their assault rifles appearing everywhere as they swept the home. Once the cottage had been thoroughly searched, and with no sign of their suspect, they deemed it secure for the detectives to enter the house and speak to Rebecca.

'WHAT THE BLOODY HELL IS GOING ON?' she screamed at the two detectives as they asked her if she knew where her husband was. Her body shook with nerves and adrenaline. 'Tell me what all this is about! You've just scared us all half to death,' she demanded, as the girls sat sobbing and still clinging onto their mother.

'We have reason to believe your husband is the man responsible for the spate of murders over the past few months, Mrs Lee, and we desperately need to locate him and ask him some questions. So I will ask you again, do you know where we can find him?'

Rebecca sat in shock and disbelief and was struggling to process what she had just heard, and ordered the children to their rooms; she didn't want them witnessing the detectives sullying their father's good name, but also wanted to find out more of what made them suspect Charles, without her daughters being in the room.

The girls did as instructed and Rebecca, now realising that there wasn't a threat towards them, informed the detectives that they were obviously mistaken and went on to state how Charles is a decent, loving family man and a God-fearing Christian who would never harm another human being.

The detectives knew there and then that Rebecca didn't have a clue about Charles' extracurricular activities.

One of them stepped in to speak to her. 'I'm sorry, Mrs Lee, I know this must be a shock to you. We've found a fingerprint at the scene of one of the murders, Haywood farm, which belonged to Mr and Mrs Beattie before Mr Beattie's murder. The fingerprint matched your husband's. We know Charles stayed with the Beatties as a child in the care system, and we know that he was formerly known as Jonathon McMullen.'

None of this made any sense whatsoever to Rebecca. She explained to them how they have obviously made a huge mistake, and that her husband has always been Charles Lee and he was never in care!

The detectives were staggered by how little she really knew about her husband's past, and could sense that she was overwhelmed with hearing this conflicting news and was adamant that they were wrong.

'I know this is hard to take in, Mrs Lee, but if there is any way whatsoever you can help us find him it would be extremely helpful. We are worried he may be about to strike again and want to bring an end to all of this; with any luck, you may be right and we can rule out any involvement from your husband and move on with our investigation. But at this moment in time, everything suggests that he has something to do with it, so it is imperative that you cooperate with us at this time.'

Rebecca, now trying to gain some composure after what had just happened and the news she had just received, began to speak, her voice breathless and hesitant. 'Ch-Charles has gone away on business for the weekend. I did think he'd been acting strange lately, but I was beginning to suspect that he was having an affair, not going around killing people! E-especially not young girls, as the ch-children couldn't wish for a better father. I... 'm sorry...I still can't believe that my husband is the man you're looking for. It's hard to think that the man I've loved all these years — the father of my children — could actually be a complete m-monster!'

'Sorry to press, Mrs Lee, but unfortunately time is of the essence, so can I ask you if you know where he has gone?' one of the detectives asked in an apologetic manner, as they could see she was nearing breakdown.

'I have no idea, Detective,' she replied. 'I didn't even know he was going away this weekend till he mentioned it just recently — he has been so secretive lately! It was the same the last time he went away.'

'Last time, Mrs Lee?'

'Yes...he said he was on a course not so long ago, again at short notice.'

The detectives then dug deeper and asked her for the date he was away the last time. When she told them, they knew instantly that it was the same night James Beattie had been murdered and knew they had definitely found the man they had been tirelessly searching for. They then asked her if she could phone Charles and maybe get him to tell her where he was so they could go there and pick him up.

She did as they had instructed but it was to be of no use as the phone instantly went to voicemail, probably due to his mobile being switched off. She tried a few more times over the next five minutes as the detectives anxiously hoped for a break, but it wasn't to be, as it was the same result every time she tried.

'Is there anybody you can think of that might know his whereabouts then, Mrs Lee?' the detective pressed.

Rebecca immediately thought of Linda, of how Charles possibly having an affair was more plausible than him being a serial murderer. If she had the pick between the choice of two evils, in a strange way she hoped she was right; it would be far easier to forgive him an affair than the alternative, even though she knew that would be devastating too.

She went and got Linda's details from Charles' home records and called the number. After a few rings a voice answered that she instantly recognised as Linda.

'Hello?'

'Oh hi, Linda, it's Rebecca here. I was just wondering if you happened to know where Charles is, as I've been trying to reach him and his phone appears to be turned off. I don't suppose he is with you is he?'

Linda thought it strange that Rebecca was calling her on a Saturday afternoon at home, but found it stranger that she was asking if Charles was with her, as he would have no reason to be.

'No, I'm afraid I can't help you with that, Rebecca. I haven't seen much of Charles lately if truth be told. Is everything ok?'

Rebecca, not wanting to let on her real reason for calling, and not wanting to start crying over the phone, assured Linda that everything was fine, said goodbye and hung up. She believed that she was not with Charles; she was momentarily pleased, but she thought that there may be something in what she had just been told.

The detectives then thanked Rebecca and asked her if there was anybody she could go and stay with, as they did not want to leave her and the kids alone in case Charles was to return and harm them. She assured them that Charles would never hurt her or the girls, but agreed that she did not want to stay there until it was all over, and arranged to go and stay at her parents with the two girls. The detectives agreed that it was for the best, then gathered their team of officers and left the property.

Little did they know that Charles was currently sat beaming in Haywood Farm as he watched Messenger slowly come round from the anaesthetic, groggily trying to make sense of what was happening to him. The Chief Inspector's eyes widened and panic started to set in as he realised he was bound and gagged, with nobody knowing his location; he knew he was surely going to die.

***

Taylor was frantically searching the city for any clues or signs that might let him know where Charles and Messenger may possibly be. He headed to the veterinary practice, and after realising that was empty, he headed next to where Amber Thompson's body was recovered from the river Eden — still nothing. He thought, it is going to be too late and Messenger may already be dead, and Charles, knowing that the police are on to him, may manage to elude them and disappear without a trace, as he had managed to do when he left the name Jonathon McMullen in the past and assumed a new identity, one that not even his family knew of. He was totally at a loss and frustrated, and decided to once again return to the hospital and speak to Georgie.

***

Charles had been extremely busy, painstakingly punishing Messenger for his sins. He started again by taking out his Stanley knife and cutting the man's Achilles tendons as he had done with Jim before to stop him from running on the off chance he was to wriggle free. He then removed the tape that covered Messenger's mouth so he could speak. Despite pain and fear, Messenger tried to remain calm and in control.

'You won't get away with this you know!' he spat at

Charles. 'You are going to get caught for what you've done. My team know exactly where we are and will already be on their way.'

Charles laughed at Messenger's attempt to try and intimidate and scare him, as he had done many times when he was a youngster. He swung his arm and heavily slapped Messenger with the back of his hand. 'SHUT THE FUCK UP! Nobody knows you're here, you piece of shit. It's just you, me and him upstairs! You have committed many a sin, Chief Inspector, and the Good Lord has deemed it your time to be judged.'

Charles was totally absorbed in his warped state of justice, with vengeance very much at the forefront of his thoughts. He picked up the Stanley knife once more and prised open Messenger's jaw with his hand. Grabbing his tongue with his other hand, he proceeded to slice the end of his tongue off with the blade so he could not offer any more bullshit. Messenger screamed but, with nobody around to hear, Charles just laughed at the man.

'That's just the beginning...' he taunted Messenger.

He grabbed the pliers he had packed and started to remove Messenger's teeth one by one. After he became bored of extracting his teeth Charles reached for the blow torch he had brought; removing Messenger's boots, he fired up the torch and proceeded to take it to the soles of his feet. As the stench of burning flesh filled the air, Charles then decided he was going to mutilate the man's genitals, just as he had with Jim. He took the torch away from Messenger's feet and kindly offered him a few minutes respite — he didn't want him passing out due to the pain.

***

Georgie breathed a sigh of relief as Taylor approached her, as she had been worrying all day about him being hurt by either Charles Lee or Chief Inspector Messenger.

'I take it there is no sign of them then?' she asked him.

'No, they have totally vanished, Georgie, and I don't know what to do or where to go from here. I was kind of hoping that you may be able to offer some of your expert advice, as I'm at a dead end.'

Georgie tried to suggest maybe he left it alone now, as the news was out about Charles and it was probably only a matter of time before the police located him and placed him in custody. Taylor was having none of it; although he had put in a lot of hard work and effort in the hunt for Charles, he desperately still wanted to be the one that brought not only him into custody, but also to be the one that placed Messenger under arrest and read him his rights before informing him of the charges brought against him — including the attempted murder of his witness. He could not leave the Chief Inspector to be brutally murdered by Charles Lee; Messenger needed to be brought to justice! Taylor now detested the man he had previously admired, and badly wanted him to pay for his crimes.

Georgie, sensing that Taylor had no intention of giving up, suggested that he re-trace Charles' previous crimes, starting at the place where Amber was found. When Taylor informed her that he had already done so, and that he had been to the practice, Georgie said something that immediately grabbed his attention:

'Maybe you should go right back to the very beginning, and go over every little piece of evidence we have, and see if we are missing something.'

'What did you just say?'

'I said, you should go back to the beginning.'

Before she could finish her sentence, he leapt out of his seat excitedly. 'You're brilliant, Georgie!' he exclaimed.

She hadn't a clue of what he meant and shouted after him, 'WHAT DO YOU MEAN?'

He raced down the long corridor and made his

way to the exit, shouting over his shoulder, 'THE BEGINNING, GEORGIE. JIM BEATTIE'S FARM, WHERE THE MURDERS STARTED!'

Georgie finally clicked. Oh yes, she thought to herself, Haywood farm would be abandoned now, and a perfect place to take Messenger!

***

As Taylor ran out of the building and through the carpark towards where he was parked, he now realised that he was heading blindly into the unknown, unarmed and alone. Knowing full well the extremities Charles was capable of, he realised that he couldn't place himself at such a high risk — he needed some back up for support. Knowing who he could trust, he called the officer who had given him the information on Charles and instructed him to send a team of his staff to oversee the armed response unit who would accompany them to Haywood farm, and stressed that he wanted Charles alive. He then raced out of the car park but, without any lights or sirens in his hire car, he had to weave in and out of traffic as he headed out of Carlisle and continued the twelve miles to Haywood farm. Taylor's heart raced with nervous anticipation and fear of what he was about to walk into, but carried on regardless; he was determined that today would be the day it would all come to an end.

***

Charles was now burning through Messenger's trousers with the blow torch. Charles' smile grew as the trousers tore and the smell of burning flesh permeated the air. The flame singed the Chief Inspector's pubic hair and blistered his genitals. Messenger desperately tried to pull away from the flame and wriggle free but it was to be no use; his restraints held out and he had to undergo this agonising torture that was befalling him.

Charles was so engrossed in his work that he failed to hear Taylor's car coming up the lane towards the farm over the stifled screaming coming from Messenger. As Taylor exited the vehicle at the rear of the farm, he spotted Charles' hidden Volvo in the barn and knew he must be inside. He steadied his nerves; he was still alone with no back up in sight.

He contemplated waiting a bit longer, but decided against it and headed towards the back door. He quietly, nervously tried the handle, trying to remain unnoticed, but the door was locked. He looked over to the broken window where Charles had let himself in; as he carefully opened it he could hear Messenger's cries coming from within the house and realised he was not too late. He tried to remain as silent as possible as he climbed through the window and set foot inside the dining room.

It suddenly dawned on him at this stage that Charles would undoubtedly have some form of weapon at his disposal, and he knew he was using it to great effect at that moment — the piercing screams became unbearable to listen to. Taylor frantically scanned the room for any kind of object that he could use against Charles in the eventuality that he came under attack. He eventually settled on a large brass fire poker, as he made his way towards the hallway and nearer to where he had just heard the screams.

The screaming subsided slightly as the detective neared the entrance to the sitting room, as Charles had removed the blow torch from what was once Messenger's genitals. He could hear Charles saying something to Messenger, but couldn't quite make out what was being said, so he cautiously made his way closer to the door to get a clearer picture of what he was saying.

He heard Charles quietly saying something to Messenger before speaking out in a loud tone, 'BUT

THERE WERE FALSE PROPHETS ALSO AMONG THE PEOPLE, EVEN AS THERE SHALL BE FALSE TEACHERS AMONG YOU, WHO PRIVILY SHALL BRING IN DAMNABLE HERESIES, EVEN DENYING THE LORD THAT BROUGHT THEM, AND BRING UPON THEMSELVES SWIFT DESTRUCTION. AND MANY SHALL FOLLOW THEIR PERNICIOUS WAYS; BY REASON OF WHOM THE WAY OF TRUTH SHALL BE EVIL SPOKEN OF. AND THROUGH COVETNOUS SHALL THEY WITH FEIGNED WORDS MAKE MERCHANDISE OF YOU: WHOSE JUDGEMENT NOW OF A LONG TIME LINGERETH NOT, AND THEIR DAMNATION SLUMBERETH NOT!'

Taylor didn't have a clue what any of what he had just heard meant, but he knew it wasn't good, and knew at that moment that he had to act, and fast, as by the sound of things Charles was preparing to kill the Chief Inspector. He decided in that instance to make his presence known and try and reason with Charles before it was too late. Taylor raised the poker aloft and threw open the sitting room door.

Charles looked up, startled, as he was just about to slice open Messenger's throat like he had done to his Social worker, Brian Jenkins.

'PLEASE, CHARLES — STOP!'

Charles stared right through him with blood-crazed eyes.

'I know why you are doing this, but please, let me do this the right way and take him in before it is too late and I won't be able to help you.'

Taylor knew what Charles had done, and rightly hated him because of this, but he also knew what it was that had driven him to this, and pleaded again for him to stop. It was at this point that they all heard the approaching sirens becoming louder and clearer, indicating the ever nearing presence of back up and the armed response unit.

Charles didn't know whether to stay and finish the job or to try and make a run for it, as he knew in that moment that everything he loved and held dear was going to be lost forever when the details finally emerged of what he had done. He angrily paced the floor with his hands on each side of his head, one still containing the knife.

Taylor again tried to reason with him, and stated that killing Messenger wouldn't undo all the wrongs he had done to him, and informed Charles that no matter what he decided to do, he would still be arresting him and taking him into custody today.

Messenger, sensing he was going to make it out alive, looked at Charles first, then Taylor, and smirked as if to say, 'I'm going to walk away from this.'

Taylor thought to himself that he possibly would; due to the torture and mental anguish he had received, he would probably be deemed too unfit to stand trial due to his mental state after undergoing this traumatic ordeal. He had to think fast as he could hear the screeching brakes of several police vehicles coming to a halt just outside of the farm. Taylor looked over where Messenger was sat partially grinning, and he made his decision.

'FUCK IT, FINISH HIM, CHARLES, BUT MAKE IT QUICK — IN ABOUT THIRTY SECONDS WE ARE GOING TO BE SURROUNDED BY ARMED RESPONSE.'

Charles needed no further encouragement, and Messenger just looked at Taylor in complete shock and disbelief as Charles grabbed him by his hair and ran his blade right through Messenger's jugular and across his throat. Taylor held his ex-boss' gaze throughout. Taylor, hearing the shouts of 'ARMED POLICE' as the team entered the house, politely asked Charles to drop the knife, turn around and place his hands behind his back.

Charles was slightly hesitant. Taylor sensed the urgency.

'Please, Charles. Just do as I ask before they storm in here and place a bullet in your forehead for what you've done!'

Charles decided to do as the detective had asked and dropped the blade, then turned his back to him and sank to his knees. He offered his hands to Taylor, who quickly placed cuffs on the man.

'DON'T SHOOT. We're coming out and I have the suspect in custody! I REPEAT, DON'T SHOOT!'

Taylor proceeded to escort Charles out of the farm towards the waiting crowd of police officers, detectives, and of course, the Armed Response Unit. He insisted that he be the one to bring him into the station, and assured Charles that no harm would come to him. Over the next forty-eight hours that Charles was kept in in custody at Carlisle police station, the only person Charles would speak to was Taylor, as he somewhat trusted him and agreed that he would speak to him, and him alone, if they wanted to know the whereabouts of the two missing girls.

***

A media frenzy was gathering outside, as news of the suspect being detained was released to the nation, with reporters desperately trying to be the first ones to discover who the mystery suspect was.

Charles opened up to Taylor about everything, and went into great length in describing the horrific abuse he had been subjected to as a child growing up on the Beatties' farm. He stipulated, though, that Edna never played any part in any of the abuse, and lived in fear of her husband so therefore never spoke up about any of the goings on at the farm.

Taylor sympathised somewhat with Charles regarding his reasoning for going after Jim, Brian and Chief Inspector Messenger. He could not, however, understand his reasons for targeting the three girls, after he had admitted that he did indeed abduct and kill the other two. Taylor could only sit and listen in disgust as Charles broke down and explained in graphic detail what he had done to the girls; he heard all about Charles' misguided logic and anger at his mother for giving him up and abandoning him to the life he had to endure. Charles explained that he'd never intended to commit any of his despicable crimes, and it wasn't until after his chance encounter with Jim towards the end of last year that all these strong feelings of hate and resentment towards her, that he must have locked away deep in his subconscious for all these years, had resurfaced and engulfed and consumed his every waking thought.

Fighting through the tears he went on to state how deeply ashamed he was of himself, and hadn't realised in doing what he had done he was no better than the men who had abused him until after killing Jim. Killing the three girls was the only thing he regretted in all of this. He then co-operated fully in helping Taylor and his staff locate the missing bodies of Lucy Mitchell and Sarah Davidson so that the parents could finally lay their daughters to rest.

He thought of his own daughters; they would now never want anything to do with him ever again. He then thought of his wife, the woman he had loved and lied to for all these years about his real background and upbringing. Maybe if he had just been honest with her from the start he might have been able to lay all his demons to rest without the need for any of this to have happened. But he knew it was too late, and that the damage was irreversible, and knew once again he would be abandoned and left alone by the ones he loved.

***

With Messenger dead, and Taylor reinstated by the new interim Chief Inspector, he thought it about time that Georgie brought in their witness after she had been released from the hospital. The witness managed to provide enough evidence of Messenger's involvement in the paedophile network to tarnish his reputation for good, even after his death, and she also managed to identify and make statements about lots of other high-ranking officials. One by one, the police arrested and charged numerous men involved in the systematic abuse of young children spanning over a total of thirty years.

After extensive psycho evaluation Charles was diagnosed as having a psychotic personality disorder, along with schizophrenia — probably brought on by the traumas of losing his parents Vicky and William McMullen at such a young age, being abused at the farm, and the death of his friend and commanding officer, Marcus Lancaster, not to mention his Post Traumatic Stress Disorder. It was ruled that Charles was not of sound mental health when he had committed his crimes; he was sectioned under the Mental Health Act and detained indefinitely at Berkshire Broadmoor Hospital for the Criminally Insane, where he would stay for the remainder of his life, with no chance of ever being released.

***

Now the case had finally been brought to an end, Georgie decided that the time was now right for her to return home and leave Taylor. He'd been promoted to the position of Chief Inspector after Messenger's demise, and was doing a fantastic job in his new role. They warmly embraced as though they had been friends for years as they said their goodbyes; a lot had happened over such a relatively short period of time. Taylor once again thanked her for all her help and repeated how he could have never done it without her support.

'You were pretty awesome yourself, mister!' she told him. 'I suppose I'll miss you. I'll definitely keep in touch from time to time to see how you're getting on, Chief Inspector!'

They very nearly came close to a kiss as they

embraced but both stopped themselves, knowing what happened the last time.

Georgie whispered in his ear, 'We'll always have the memory of our night together.'

They finally ended their embrace. Taylor could only smile as he watched her walk away, get into her car, and drive out of his life.

***

A month had passed since Charles had been admitted to Broadmoor and the media circus was starting to die down; journalists were beginning to run out of stories to tell regarding Charles' background, the abuse and, of course, his victims. It was at this point that Rebecca finally felt the time was right to visit Charles.

She could barely look him in the eye as she sat and explained that, since what he had done had come to light, she and the girls had received nothing but abuse from everybody they had encountered. He had made their lives unbearable, with even so-called close friends turning their backs on them. She went on to say how the girls had disowned him for what he had done and put them through, and never wished to see him again for the rest of their lives; they couldn't bear the thought that their father, the man they loved and idolised, was actually a monster. She then told him that this would be the last time he would ever see her or the girls as she couldn't take any more. She was going to stay with distant relatives in Canada and start a new life for her and the girls, and possibly assume new identities to escape being linked to him.

Charles could not find any words to say to his wife and just sat there in tears, ashamed of what he had done, of what he had put them through. He knew that she meant every word of what she had just told him; he would never see her again. She just had one last question to ask him before she got up and turned to leave.

'Was everything a lie, Charles — or should I say, Jonathon? Did you ever love me and the girls, or was it just all a cover up?'

Tears ran down his face as he replied. 'I have loved you from the very first day I saw you back in that corridor at Lancaster. And I shall love you, Molly and Fiona until the day I die, Rebecca. I know you will never understand what I have done, and I don't expect you or the girls to, but please know, and let them know, that I will always love you three, and I will miss you every day until the Good Lord hands me my judgement.'

Rebecca held back her tears just long enough to get out of sight of Charles, then broke down as she realised he had meant every word he had just spoke. Part of her still loved Charles, despite what he had done, but part of her knew that she had never really known him — she never knew about all the hurt and suffering he had been through. She pitied him and, even though she could never get their old life back, she promised herself that she would remember him in her prayers every night. She found herself hoping that one day he would finally find peace and comfort from his demons, and find it in his heart to forgive all the people who had ever wronged him. With that, she left the hospital grounds and never looked back.

Charles was heartbroken and devastated as he was escorted back to his cell, and once again broke down in despair and prayed to the Lord for help and guidance. But, whereas before he'd believed God had somehow guided him in what he was doing, now he felt nothing. He was abandoned by not only his family, but by the one person he thought he could rely on in times of crisis and despair, ever since he first picked up the Bible as a child. He didn't know which way to turn, and could not see a way out of his torture.

Once he had managed to gain some form of composure he finally decided he knew what he had to do...he would be committing a mortal sin by doing so, but his God had already decided to cast him aside! He decided he was going to take his own life.

He tore his sheet from his bed into thin strips of material, stood on his stool and tied one of the ends to the light fitting that was positioned above him in the centre of the room. Once he had secured it into position he thought about writing a long letter to his wife and children to try and justify his previous actions, but decided against it; he knew it wouldn't matter what he was to say, as he had caused them too much suffering to forgive. Instead he took a thick grey crayon he had been deemed safe to use, and started to write on the bright white cell wall.

CAN A WOMAN FORGET HER SUCKING CHILD, THAT SHE SHOULD NOT HAVE COMPASSION ON THE SON OF HER WOMB? YEA, THEY MAY FORGET, YET I WILL NOT FORGET THEE.

Charles took one last look at the words he had written, then stood on his stool, slipped the noose he had prepared on the other end of the sheet around his neck, then uttered the words, 'God, please forgive me.'

He kicked the stool from under him and felt the strain of the noose as it tightened around his neck. Charles didn't even bother to fight it; his mind was firmly made up. A solitary tear ran down his cheek as he thought of happier times with Rebecca and the children. He hoped they would one day meet again in the afterlife. The last flicker of life exited his body and his existence was extinguished.

***

In one very last cruel twist of fate, a letter arrived the following day, addressed to Charles.

Charles, by this time, had been discovered dead in his cell. The governor decided to open the letter

209

and see if there was a return address. He found the sender's details at the top right of the page; a Mrs Shelley Winter from Silloth in Cumbria. The governor couldn't help but read the contents through morbid curiosity.

Dear Charles,

You will not know who I am, but I know you. I've been meaning to contact you for so many years I've lost count; I just never found the right words to say. The simple truth is: I am your birth mother.

I'm so, so sorry to hear of the horrific upbringing you received as a child. I read all about it in the papers after your arrest. I could've prevented all of this from happening. I regret giving you up every day of my life — I was forced to by my parents, but I should've somehow forced them to see sense. I've searched for you for years with no luck — who knew that, all that time, we had been living on each other's doorstep? I even kept my maiden name to make it easier for you to find me, even though I've been married for many years now.

Yes, I married your father! We grew up and decided that the time was right for us to be reunited. You even have a little brother and sister now! I hope you can one day meet them, no matter the circumstances. I never spoke to my parents after leaving home and starting my own life. I cannot forgive them for making me abandon you.

However, I do beg your forgiveness for what I let them do to me, to us. Please write back. Please forgive me.

With all my love, always,
Your mother
xxx

Author Profile

In this potentially controversial new psychological thriller *Abandoned* we are introduced to first time novelist Lee shepherd.

After spending years writing in his spare time, producing anything from poetry to children's stories for his own two children, he decided that the time was finally right to attempt to fulfil his life-long ambition of creating a full length novel.

Lee lives in Carlisle in the heart of Cumbria, having moved north from Lancashire in his mid-teens; he has a first-hand knowledge of all the areas mentioned in *Abandoned*, and now calls this idyllic setting home.

Although Lee one day dreams of becoming a full time author and screen play writer, he currently spends the majority of his working week caring for and mentoring teenagers in care as a Child Support Worker throughout Scotland.

His hobbies include snooker, boxing, fishing and working out in his local gym whenever the rare opportunity of down time presents itself, in between being a father and a husband to his wife, Kelly.

For all enquiries and feedback you can contact Lee at leeshepherdl980@gmail.com

Publisher Information

Rowanvale Books provides publishing services to independent authors, writers and poets all over the globe. We deliver a personal, honest and efficient service that allows authors to see their work published, while remaining in control of the process and retaining their creativity. By making publishing services available to authors in a cost-effective and ethical way, we at Rowanvale Books hope to ensure that the local, national and international community benefits from a steady stream of good quality literature.

For more information about us, our authors or our publications, please get in touch.

www.rowanvalebooks.com
info@rowanvalebooks.com